# a hole in the world

## sid hite

SCHOLASTIC 📖 SIGNATURE

an imprint of
## SCHOLASTIC INC.
New York  Toronto  London  Auckland  Sydney
Mexico City  New Delhi  Hong Kong  Buenos Aires

MANY THANKS TO MY PERSPICACIOUS EDITOR, TRACY MACK,

WHO MADE INNUMERABLE WELL-REASONED SUGGESTIONS THAT

GREATLY ENHANCED THE TELLING OF THIS STORY.


ALSO THANKS TO LESLIE BUDNICK, WHO CHEERFULLY HANDLES

ALL THE TRICKY STUFF AROUND THE OFFICE.

ISBN 0-439-09831-9

12 11 10 9 8 7 6 5 4 3 2          2 3 4 5 6 7/0

Printed in the U.S.A.          40

First Scholastic paperback printing, October 2002

The display type was set in Sand.
The text type was set in 10-point Garamond Light.

Book design by Marijka Kostiw

TO HAVE DIED ONCE IS ENOUGH.

*Virgil*

LET THE GENTLE, KINDLY PHANTOMS

HAUNT AS THEY WILL;

WE ARE NOT AFRAID OF THEM.

*Jerome K. Jerome*

Paul Shackleford glared angrily from the passenger window of the car that carried him farther and farther from home. He could hardly believe what was happening. Here it was, the dawn of the twenty-first century, and he'd been condemned to a summer of indentured servitude. Incredibly, his own parents had done the condemning.

Paul was a bright individual with mouse-brown hair, light brown eyes, and a distinctive dimple in his chin. He was slight of build, yet had enough muscle on his body to avoid qualifying for skinny. He was about a seven on a one-to-ten handsome scale. His

**one**

mind was quick and he had plenty of friends who appreciated his lively sense of humor. Paul was already painfully aware that he would miss these friends dearly during the weeks and months of his summer-long exile.

Paul's father, Morris Shackleford, earned his living as a lawyer. Even so, he was a likable person, and under normal circumstances he and Paul got along pretty well. However, there was nothing normal about the current situation, which had father and son locked

in a battle of wills. It was a battle that recent history said the son was bound to lose. Still, Paul put up a fight, vainly attempting to conquer his father with the sheer power of barbed thoughts. Paul should have saved his energy or dispensed it in other ways, for Morris Shackleford simply retreated behind a wall of indifference and hummed show tunes under his breath.

Finally, more than an hour out of Richmond, after

failing to make so much as a dent in Morris's mood, Paul abandoned his silent attack and resorted to words. "Dad, this is absurd. Just because I made one small error of judgment, you have no right to cut me off from the world."

Morris ceased humming. "I assure you, son, the Vallenports live in the world. The only thing you'll be cut off from is a familiar environment."

"You know what I mean."

"I do, but it doesn't negate what I said."

Paul groaned. It was never easy arguing with a lawyer — especially one who doubled as a father. Nevertheless, Paul's entire summer was on the line, and he wasn't ready to concede defeat. "I'm trying to be serious, Dad, and you're acting like an A-ONE FAT-HEAD. You always tell me to listen when you speak, but you won't even consider what I'm saying."

Morris smiled. "Go ahead, speak. I'll listen. But first, a word to the wise. When you wish to persuade someone resistant to your line of thinking, you ought not call him a fathead before you start."

"Sorry about that," Paul offered quickly. "I happen to be upset."

Morris's smile became a grin. "Apology accepted. Now let's hear your appeal."

"Okay." Paul took a breath and released tension from his body. "To begin with, I'm fifteen and old enough to learn from my mistakes. I get good grades in school and am not a delinquent. You have to admit, except for this recent incident, I've never given you or Mom much trouble."

"No, you haven't."

"Good, you agree. And I admit it was stupid of me trying to protect a friend by lying, and even stupider because the person I lied for wasn't really my friend in the first place. So there. I learned my lesson, and I swear I'll never lie on someone's behalf again."

"That's easily said now, isn't it? If I recall correctly,

you swore to me when I asked about this matter that you weren't lying."

Paul grimaced. "I wasn't thinking then. I was reacting to getting caught."

Morris made a face that said: *my point exactly*.

Paul heaved an exasperated sigh. Like anyone in his right mind, he did not enjoy being branded as a liar. In fact, he was usually pretty good at sticking to the truth. "Dad, I know what you and Mom are doing. You think my spending a summer with a bunch of hokey old farmers will teach me about honesty. But I just told you I've learned that lesson . . . which means there's no need to follow through on this. Let's just stop and call the Vallenports. You can explain that I'm not coming."

Morris snorted. "I suggest you add humility and respect to your list of lessons, son. Those hokey old farmers are apt to be smarter than you think."

"I didn't say they were dumb."

"No, but you implied you were better than them, and that reflects the arrogance that got you into this mess to begin with. School smarts are one thing, yet they don't equal the wisdom that comes with maturity."

"You think I'm immature? Is that why you're punishing me?"

"I'm not sending you away as punishment."

"NO? It sure feels that way to me."

"You are old enough to learn from your mistakes. In a few years you'll make all your own decisions and be responsible for yourself. Meanwhile, it's my job to prepare you for that day. I believe you need to broaden your perspective, to learn that Richmond isn't the start and end of the universe."

Paul rolled his eyes and resumed glaring out the window. Deep down, he was fond of Morris and knew the man was just doing his fatherly best. Paul also knew — punishment or no punishment — that he had gotten himself into this mess.

Referring now and then to handwritten directions, Morris drove west and slightly north from Richmond and proceeded deeper and deeper into the countryside. He and Paul were headed to a farm belonging to Ada and Hargrove Vallenport. Ada Vallenport was the daughter of the oldest son of one of Paul's mother's great-aunts on her father's side. (Paul had reportedly met Ada and Hargrove thirteen years before when the couple attended a wedding in Richmond and stayed at his parents' home, but he was a two-year-old riot in diapers at the time and retained no memory of the meeting.) The Vallenports were hardly close kin, and yet they were ostensibly doing a family favor by taking Paul for the summer. He had a radically different view of the situation. As far as Paul was concerned, the Vallenports were veritable strangers who had conspired with his parents to usurp his freedom.

Paul and Morris eventually entered Spring County and passed through the three-block burg of Fenton,

Virginia. From his window, Paul saw two people sitting in a diner and a dog lying in a pool of shade on Main Street. His mood grew glummer when Morris informed him that Fenton was nine miles from the Vallenports' farm and was the main megalopolis in the county.

They turned left at the north end of town, crossed a set of railroad tracks, and followed a winding road through a seemingly endless swell of rolling hills. The farther they drove, the more apprehensive Paul grew. For all the eye to see, there was nothing but woods, fields, more woods, and every so often, a farm.

The pair soon arrived at a gate at the foot of a long driveway. The drive led up a steeply sloped field to a three-story, brick house. Paul hopped out and opened the gate, then closed it, got back in the car, and eyed the hilltop home. Four white columns supported a roof over a brick veranda in front of the house. There were dark green shutters on the windows. A single tall tree stood in the front yard, and here and there, a few bushes. Otherwise the hilltop was bare.

They pulled into a gravel lot and parked between a tractor and a battered, old green pickup. Out of the corner of his eye Paul saw a tan-colored, barrel-chested dog intently observing the car's arrival. "Dad, are you sure?"

Morris laughed. "It won't be so bad. Who knows? You might like farming and thank me later for bringing you here."

"I might get struck by lightning too."

Morris switched off the engine. "Son, I know you think I'm being unreasonable. Maybe I am, but you're here now, so you might as well make the most of the experience."

Paul shrugged. What could he do but acquiesce?

Then Morris surprised Paul by saying, "Listen. The Fourth of July is little more than three weeks away. You'll come home for a visit then. If at that time you really can't stand the idea of returning here, I won't make you come back."

Although the look on Paul's face implied that he was shocked, his voice conveyed appreciation. "That's fair enough. Thanks, Dad."

"Sure," said Morris. "Now, one last thing. Have you ever heard the saying 'To the desert is the jungle real?'"

Paul shook his head.

"Well, think about it before you judge the people you're going to meet. From their point of view, you're the oddball for living in a city."

Paul indicated with a nod that he would consider the saying, then opened the passenger-side door, stepped from the car, and started toward the trunk to fetch his belongings. Before he could get there, the dog that had watched the Shacklefords' arrival completed its dash across the parking lot and snapped at Paul's rear end. It was an instructive nip, no harm done. All the same, Paul jumped, whirled, and fell back against the car. The dog stood several feet away, looked Paul squarely in the eye, and growled. The creature's message was clear: *I'm top dog on this farm. Don't you forget.*

As Paul cowered against the car and wondered why the dog had come after him instead of Morris, a woman emerged from the back of the house. She had coal-black eyes and an abundance of dark hair gathered into a loosely arranged bun. "Einstein," the woman shouted, wagging a finger at the dog, "get away from my guests this instant."

The dog glanced at the woman, threw a warning look at Paul, then went to lie down under the nearby pickup.

The woman proceeded across the parking lot. "Morris, nice to see you. It's been far too long."

"Hello, Ada. You're looking well."

"And you," the woman replied as she continued forward. Paul could see a few smatterings of gray in her hair, yet did not get the impression that she was elderly. Indeed, her bearing was straight, her figure firm, and her movements sure, and (Paul thought) she had a pleasantly attractive face. "So sorry about the rude welcome," she addressed Paul in a heavily lilted, almost musical accent. "Einstein only does that to first-time visitors. You must be Paul."

"Yes, ma'am."

"I'm Ada Vallenport."

"Nice to meet you, ma'am," Paul replied politely. Upset though he might be, he was not the type to forget his manners.

Ada Vallenport paused a moment and studied Paul closely. He got the strange impression that she was perplexed, or perhaps disappointed by what she saw. Soon, though, her face broke into a warm smile and she told Paul, "You can relax. Einstein won't attack again. And neither will I."

Paul understood that Ada Vallenport was trying to

make him feel welcome and forced a weak smile onto his face. "No, ma'am. I'm not worried . . . I was just startled by the dog."

"As anyone would be. Come, let's get your stuff and go in. Morris, you're staying for dinner, I hope."

"Thank you, Ada, but no. I promised Louise that I'd get back as soon as I could. We made plans to go out."

"You'll come in for coffee, won't you? Or tea?"

"Oh, yes." Morris smiled. "I always have time for coffee."

"And for driving your son to prison," Paul mumbled sarcastically.

"What?" said Morris.

"Nothing," Paul replied as he reached into the trunk for his bags. "Just thinking to myself, that's all."

Paul and Morris were greeted at the rear door by Hargrove Vallenport, who gave them each a hardy handshake, then led them to the parlor while Ada went to get coffee for Morris and ice tea for Paul. Hargrove was a portly man with a proud nose, a high forehead, thinning hair, and a bum left leg that caused him to limp. Although a good decade older than Paul's father, and despite his handicap, Hargrove exuded an air of strength and vitality. He ushered the guests into a carpeted, lamp-lit den and introduced them to Ada's white-haired mother. "Frances," Hargrove said in a

**two**

crisp voice. "This is Morris Shackleford and his son, Paul. Gentlemen, this is Frances Furr."

"How do you do?" The woman peered at Morris and Paul through thick, round glasses that magnified the size of her eyes.

"Fine, thanks," said Morris, and Paul echoed the sentiment. The old woman reminded him of a snowy, white owl.

"Glad to see we're all well," Frances quipped with a rubbery smile and rested her gaze on Paul. "You call me Granny. Everyone else does. And sit there where I can get a good look at you. You might just remind me of someone I once knew."

While Hargrove and Morris made small talk about the area's booming real estate prices and Granny Furr scrutinized Paul, Ada asked her young guest a few casual questions, such as "What grade are you in?" "Do you enjoy sports?" and "Have you spent time in the country before?" Although Paul answered each question politely, he did so monosyllabically and without enthusiasm. Prior to this moment he'd been so busy resisting his fate, he'd not seriously considered the details of what it might entail, and now he was bummed. The people in the house where he was condemned to reside were four times his own age on average.

He made a quick calculation in his head. There were twenty-two days and twenty-three nights between now and the Fourth of July. That was at least twenty days longer than Paul figured he might survive.

In due time Morris finished his coffee, said goodbye to Hargrove, Ada, and Granny, and prepared to depart. Paul followed his father into the hallway and out through the door by which they'd entered the big house. They stopped in the parking lot, and, while Paul kept his eyes on the dog named Einstein, they said their adieus.

"Take care, son. Your mother and I will miss you."

"You wouldn't if I rode home with you now."

Morris chortled. "See you, Paul. Call if you get lonely."

"Bye, Dad," Paul said flatly, and as he watched his father get in his car and drive away, a lump formed in his throat. It wasn't a lump of projected loneliness. It was a lump of "there's no escape now."

Approximately an hour after his father's departure, Paul stood at the window of his newly assigned, third-floor bedroom, peering out over the Vallenports' farm. It was a handsome spread, containing some twenty-nine hundred acres of gently rolling hills and fields. Earlier, in the parlor, he'd overheard Hargrove telling Morris that many of the old farms on the east side of the Blue Ridge Mountains had recently been purchased by city people and turned into white-fenced showplaces for the town and country set. This was not the case with the Vallenports. They raised cattle, corn, hay, hogs, oats, and soybeans, and depended on their land for a living. They were real farmers.

When Ada Vallenport showed Paul to his room she'd told him it afforded a particularly fine view of Gallihugh Mountain, and now as he gazed over the farm, his eye was drawn repeatedly to that solitary mass rising in the west. The isolated mountain stood alone against the sky, separate from its mother range, and somehow, abstractly, expressed much of what Paul was feeling inside.

It was nigh on six-thirty when Paul descended the two flights of stairs to the dining room where he'd been told to report for supper. As he walked into the large room he was surprised to see an unfamiliar face at the table. The face belonged to a broad-shouldered, bearded man who was about thirty years old. No one had to tell Paul who the man's parents were. He had Ada's dark hair and eyes, and though his nose was less proud than Hargrove's, he had his father's high fore-head.

Ada greeted Paul by name, tapped the chair be-tween her and Granny, then turned toward the bearded man. "This is Ellis, our son. He lives in the valley be-low and usually joins us for Sunday suppers."

Paul could feel Ellis studying him as he approached the table and sat. After the two exchanged nods, Ellis aimed a look of acknowledgment at Granny. It ap-peared to Paul that Ellis was agreeing with her on some previously discussed matter.

Dinner was not a fancy affair. Hargrove whispered a quick prayer, plates were filled with large portions, and everyone began to eat. There was little conversa-tion during the course of the meal, which suited Paul fine. All he wanted to do was eat and go back to his room.

Just about every time he looked over he found Ellis watching him or turning away from watching him. Paul was beginning to wonder if he'd grown a second nose. Between first meeting Ada in the parking lot, sitting in the parlor with Granny, and now being closely observed by Ellis, Paul felt akin to a medical specimen under a microscope. Was this how all backwoods families treated their houseguests?

Finally, toward the end of the meal, Ellis made direct eye contact with Paul and asked him bluntly, "You ever worked with your hands before?"

"A little," Paul replied meekly. "Mostly yard work. I don't know anything about farming."

Ellis paused a few seconds before replying, "There's not a lot to know. All you'll need for farming is a back, two legs, and two arms. Brains aren't required."

Paul swallowed and said nothing.

Ellis chuckled. He seemed intent on making Paul uncomfortable. "Don't worry, kid. I'll show you the ropes."

On the surface of things, it was clear to Paul that

Ellis was joking, yet at the same time there was an edge to the man's words, and Paul did not relish the prospect of learning what Ellis might have to teach him.

Ada also detected the edge and said rather tersely to Ellis, "I'm sure Paul will do fine."

"He will if he doesn't spook easily," Granny adjoined with a knowing smile and a laugh.

"Excuse me?" Paul turned to Granny. Out of the corner of his eye he saw Ellis glare at his grandmother, and before the woman could reply to Paul's query, Ellis interjected, "Don't pay Granny any mind. She often says things out of the blue."

Granny Furr quit smiling and settled her owlish eyes on Ellis. "A large part of all conversations originate in the blue. I was just being social."

"As Ellis should learn to be," Ada added, staring pointedly at her son.

Ellis crossed his hefty arms over his chest, sat back in his chair, and grinned.

Hargrove cleared the tension from the air with a cough and told Paul, "You'll have to excuse us. Wrangling over words is a popular pastime around here."

Paul dipped his head to Hargrove and shrank down in his seat. He suspected that something had just been brushed under the table, yet did not have the gumption to inquire further into the matter. Although "spooked" was too strong a word for his current state of mind, he was feeling emotionally daunted.

The end of dinner came none too quickly for Paul, who retreated upstairs as soon as was politely acceptable and sat forlornly on his bed. After moping for an hour, he went to the window and watched the darkening sky fill with stars. He was still watching when the third-quarter crescent of a waning moon floated over the horizon and lit the bolder contours of the land in a pale, silvery light.

After a while, Paul spotted Einstein sitting in the

yard, gazing up to the third-floor window. He had not seen the dog approach, nor did he know how long Einstein had been watching him, yet the peculiar canine was clearly concentrating on Paul. For several moments they peered at each other in the semidarkness, and then the barrel-chested mutt turned toward the sinking moon and howled.

*Aaouuuuu.*

*Aaouuuuu.*

After saying his piece, Einstein turned again to Paul and was quiet. Paul had half a mind to open the window and throw one of the new boots his mother had bought him at the dog. He did not. He would need both boots in the morning when he started his first day of work on the farm. He looked forward to that with all the zeal of a cat anticipating a cold bath. The way his luck was running, he feared he'd be at Ellis's beck and call all day.

"This is just great," Paul sarcastically told the moon.

"Mom and Dad should have just taken me out and shot me."

Paul remained at the window for another half hour or so, watching the dog, then drifted to the bed and sprawled out on his back. Gradually he approached dreamland. He was almost there when he heard a distant train rattling through the night. He followed the sound southward and wondered if the train was headed past his Richmond home.

Paul was again at sleep's door when a lupine call yanked him back into wakefulness.

*Aaouuuuu.* It was Einstein, imitating a wolf.

Paul grabbed a pillow, scrunched it over his head, and wished he'd caught the passing train . . . going anywhere. He didn't care.

*Aaouuuuu.*

Paul was pestered awake by the discordant crowing of a rooster. He yawned and glanced at the clock on the table by his bed. It was ten to seven, almost time to rise and meet the day.

It is not uncommon for individuals oppressed by trying circumstances to enjoy a dash of optimism at the onset of a new day. Such was the case with Paul as he slipped from bed, pulled on his jeans, and reached for his new boots. A dash of optimism, however, is a small tonic and does not constitute a complete psychological overhaul. For Paul it simply meant that he was feeling

three

a little less dreadful about his fate than he had the night before.

Paul went to the window. Down below he saw a scraggly bird strutting figure eights in the yard. Einstein was lying under a bush, casually eyeing the fowl. Paul watched the dog, expecting him to attack the rooster at any moment, but Einstein did not move, and several minutes later when the clock by Paul's bed chirped its mechanical alert, the rooster was still crowing and strutting with impunity. *Oh, well,* thought Paul. *The dog is crazy and so is the bird. And I'll be, too, after a couple of weeks on this farm.*

Paul descended the two flights of stairs and started toward the small room off the kitchen where he'd been told to report for breakfast. He encountered Hargrove in the hallway, approaching from the opposite end of the house. "Morning, son. You sleep alright?"

"Yes, sir."

"Dog didn't bother you? I heard him howling."

Paul shook his head.

Hargrove smiled knowingly, then started across the dining room toward a corner door. "Come meet the crew," he said over his shoulder to Paul.

They entered a narrow, windowless room where three, square-shouldered men sat at a metal table drinking coffee. As Paul and Ellis exchanged glances of recognition, Hargrove gestured at Paul and said, "I'd like to introduce Paul Shackleford, one of Ada's kin. He'll be helping around here for the summer."

It seemed to Paul that the two men he'd not met before did a double take when they looked in his direction. Afterward, when they turned to Ellis, there was no question about the I-told-you-so look he gave the men.

As all of this registered in Paul's mind, Hargrove was saying, "Paul, this thoughtful fellow here is Dundas Shoals. And that handsome gent sitting beside Ellis is Tucker Dyson."

Dundas Shoals nodded vaguely at Paul, and

Tucker Dyson mumbled a perfunctory hello. Paul sensed he should say something — good morning, how do you do?, anything — yet his voice stuck in his throat, and instead of speaking he stood silently in place, feeling for all the world like an innocent Cub Scout that had stumbled into a roadhouse bar.

Fortunately for the blushing, tongue-tied Paul, the kitchen door soon swung open and the men's eyes turned from him to a plump, middle-aged woman wearing a starched white apron. She had short, curly brown hair, a pug nose, a double chin, and flashing green eyes. "All right, you ingrates," she announced in a clipped tone. "Come and get it."

The men arose in unison, then hesitated when they saw the woman take notice of Paul. They watched her with smiles of anticipation, obviously curious to hear what she might say about the newcomer. Resting her hands on her hips, she methodically surveyed all five feet eight inches of Paul's physique. When her inspection was done she snorted and said, "So you're the extra hand Mrs. V. told me to expect. Good Lord, you're a skinny one. You best come in here and serve yourself a double helping of everything."

The men chuckled and filed into the kitchen. As Paul and Hargrove followed, Hargrove told Paul, "That's Inez Buttons. Whatever you do this summer, don't upset Inez."

Paul nodded, and as he did so, the last of his waking optimism dissipated within him. His only consolation at the moment was the sweet smell of hot, buttered cornbread wafting through the kitchen door.

Paul had filled his plate and was about to return to the adjoining room when Inez tapped him on the shoulder. "Hold on, son. You sit in here where I can watch you eat. Besides, we try to squeeze another chair in the nook and those heathens are liable to fight."

*Heathens?* Paul thought as Inez retrieved a stool from a corner and set it by the counter. *What century are these people living in?*

"Here. This will be your spot," said Inez. "You're looking like a beanpole now. Come the end of summer, I want folks thinking you're a man."

After Hargrove finished filling his plate and before heading into the dining room, where he regularly ate alone with his morning paper, he told Paul, "Meet you in the nook after breakfast and we'll decide what you'll be doing today."

"Yes, sir," said Paul.

Because of his bum leg, Hargrove had limited his role on the farm to conducting the post-breakfast meeting in which the day's chores were discussed and assigned. After the meeting, he usually drove to Fenton, where he spent his days manning the small real estate office he owned with a partner.

In today's meeting, Paul learned that he would spend his first day of indentured servitude in the hog house with Dundas Shoals. Paul was initially relieved with his assignment, thinking, *At least I won't be work-*

*ing with Ellis.* But after Hargrove added, "You might find the smell in there a bit mighty," Paul wasn't sure if he'd gotten lucky or not.

The crew had gotten up from their chairs and turned toward a door leading out through the garage when Ellis slapped Paul on the shoulder and advised him with a laugh, "You pay attention to Dundas. He knows all there is to know about swine."

Paul grimaced. He could not discern whether Ellis was trying to be funny or mean. Whatever the case, Dundas Shoals looked askance at Ellis and said nothing. As it was, Paul had yet to hear Dundas speak and wondered if the man even owned a voice.

After following Dundas into the parking lot, Paul witnessed a rather bizarre event, or sequence of events, that went something like this: Ellis and Tucker Dyson hopped into the cab of the old, green pickup truck, and Tucker started the motor. Then Einstein leaped from his resting spot in the flower bed beneath the kitchen window, scampered across the parking lot, placed himself in front of the truck's right front tire and started barking loudly. He obviously did not want the vehicle to go anywhere.

Tucker seemed to know Einstein would stay inches ahead of the tire and drove from the lot at approximately five miles per hour. The truck sped up to ten miles per hour . . . then to fifteen, and the whole while Einstein ran at a sort of sideways angle, barking, growling, and snapping at the offending tire. When the green vehicle reached the head of the driveway, Tucker spun the steering wheel sharply to the left and stomped the pedal to the floorboard. The truck surged into the field, swooped around in front of Einstein, and raced toward the gate at the foot of the hill.

It was then that Paul first heard Dundas speak. "The trick is to drive through the gate and close it before Einstein gets there. If you don't, he'll hem you in on the road."

Fascinated, Paul observed as the truck slid to a halt at the foot of the hill. Then Ellis jumped from the vehicle and threw open the gate, the truck roared forward, and Ellis closed the gate behind him. Einstein — arriving a nanosecond too late — slammed into the barrier and bounced sideways onto the ground.

"Now watch," advised Dundas.

At this point Paul couldn't have averted his eyes for a fifty-dollar bill.

Einstein recovered his feet and dashed for a hole beneath the fence, which he squirmed through before darting into the road and halting. For a brief moment Paul thought the dog had given up the chase, but then he understood that Einstein was waiting for the vehicle to commit itself at an upcoming fork. When the truck took the low road toward Ellis's house in the valley, Einstein bolted from the road and loped across an adjoining field in hot pursuit.

"Amazing," remarked Paul. "What's with that dog and the truck?"

"It's complicated," Dundas said and started walking.

As Paul came along beside him, he continued, "Einstein used to belong to a man named Hennley Gray, who used to work here, and that was his truck. But he's gone now and Einstein misses him. The dog, he figures whenever Hennley comes back from wherever he went, he'll go to the truck like he always did."

"Oh," said Paul. His negative first impression of Einstein notwithstanding, he had to admire the dog's fierce loyalty to his master.

"You kinda look like him."

"Who? Hennley?"

"Yep."

Paul hemmed thoughtfully, and as he and Dundas continued on foot toward the far west corner of the front field, he reflected, *Maybe that explains all the staring and the double takes.*

Dundas was somewhere in his mid-fifties. He had a squarish head, and short, barbered hair, and he observed the world through hazel-colored eyes. Those eyes, along with the strangely off-kilter expression he wore on his face, gave Paul the impression that Dundas was permanently absorbed by some abstract matter. Indeed, he reminded Paul of a man trying to solve an algebra problem in his head.

They walked all the way to the hog house. It was nearly a mile. As Dundas informed Paul, he had sworn off operating motorized vehicles after an accident in a borrowed car more than thirty years ago. The accident

four

had involved a chipmunk and a cow. Neither Dundas nor the chipmunk were injured, but the cow had gone to hamburger heaven and the borrowed car was a total loss.

Dundas fished a key from his pocket as they approached the gated fence surrounding the buildings and pens that constituted the hog house. He opened the lock, then turned to Paul and said, "I'll bet you a dollar your new boots are broken in by the end of the day."

"No, thanks. I don't usually gamble."

"That's good," noted Dundas. "I only bet on sure things."

Paul was put to work in a hundred-square-foot pen that had been recently vacated by sixty well-fed hogs. His tools were a shovel and a wheelbarrow, and his job was to rid the ground of muck. Paul wasn't offended or shocked by his assignment — he had been expecting dirty, back-bending work — but he was physically and mentally revolted by the rank, biologically active odor that permeated the air around him. Hargrove had been putting it mildly when warning that the smell in the hog house was a bit mighty. It would have been more accurate for the man to say the place stunk to high heaven, which it did.

"There's a yellow shed down that path there," Dundas told Paul. "Dump your diggings behind it. You'll see a pile already started."

"Yes, sir," Paul replied, wishing someone had advised him to bring a clothespin for his nose.

"And don't let Vanessa scare you when you go by the shed."

"Vanessa?"

"Yep," said Dundas. And without bothering to explain who or what Vanessa might be, he added, "She gets temperamental when she's expecting."

Paul nodded. He was beginning to conclude that Dundas was missing a few screws.

Paul went to work with intentions of doing a good

job and doing it fast. That was credit to his character, yet indicative of his lack of experience with manual labor. As he quickly learned, fast did not go well with shoveling pig manure (nothing does) and by the time he'd filled the wheelbarrow with his first load of muck, he already had a cramp in his left shoulder and the makings of a blister on his right hand.

During the ensuing hour, Paul was surprised by how quickly he adjusted to the foul odor that had previously threatened to overwhelm him. *If I can get used to this,* he mused, *I can get used to anything.* During the same hour he completed four trips back and forth past the yellow shed without seeing or hearing any signs of Vanessa. Finally, after depositing his fifth wheelbarrow load onto the muck pile, he decided to stop and investigate.

He parked the wheelbarrow by the shed and climbed onto the wooden gate barring the entrance. He bent at the waist, leaned forward, and craned his head into the shadowy darkness of the windowless building. It was a bold, yet foolish thing to do. Before his eyes finished adjusting to the lack of light, he heard an explosive grunt. Immediately afterward, he beheld a tan-colored, six-hundred-pound mass springing upward and whirling about in the air. The mass flew toward the gate, and Paul promptly fell from his perch into the wheelbarrow, which toppled and flung him to the ground with a thump.

Paul was still catching his breath when he heard a sniffing sound and felt a rush of warm air pass over his cheek. He rotated his head and found himself peering into the nasal chambers of a whiskered, pink snout protruding through a horizontal opening in the slated gate. The appendage twitched and strained for Paul's cheek. He was so stunned he could not move . . . not for several seconds . . . not until Dundas strolled into view and remarked, "Vanessa does that when she wants a kiss."

Paul rolled out from under her snout and picked himself up. Dundas reached through the open space in the gate, scratched the top of Vanessa's head, and pretended not to notice Paul's intense embarrassment.

Paul righted the fallen wheelbarrow and was about to return to the half-cleaned pen when he paused and asked Dundas something he'd wondered about several times that morning. "The man that owned Einstein, will he be coming back?"

"I doubt it," Dundas said with a shake of his head.

"No?" Paul sounded a curious note.

"Naw. Not Hennley. He died last year. These days he spends most of his time down in the hole with the devil."

Paul wasn't the son of a lawyer for nothing. "If he's dead, why do you say 'most of his time'?"

"Because Hennley gets out sometimes."

Paul searched Dundas's eyes for signs of facetiousness, but found none. "You mean, he gets out of the devil's hole?"

"That's right," Dundas confirmed with a nod. "Hennley always was a slick one. Knew just how to get out of jams."

"You're pulling my leg, aren't you?" Paul stared incredulously at Dundas.

Dundas said with a look that he didn't appreciate Paul doubting his word, then turned and started up the path. "Come on, son. I'll help you finish cleaning that pen."

Paul suppressed the notion to inform Dundas that he was not a gullible fool and pushed the wheelbarrow forward.

With Dundas helping, the job went three times faster, and the proscribed area was passably clean by a quarter to twelve. They were scattering sawdust over the ground when Paul heard an air horn resounding in the distance.

"Lunchtime," said Dundas.

"Hallelujah," said Paul. At this point the makings of the blister on his right hand had matured into a raw sore and the cramp in his shoulder had evolved into a dull, radiating pain.

Inez leaned against the sink with her arms crossed in front of her and beamed with delight as Paul hungrily ate his meal. "Want more beans?" she asked after Paul cleaned his plate.

"Yes, ma'am." Paul couldn't remember ever being so hungry.

"Beans come with cornbread. It's a house rule."

"I don't want to break any house rules."

"No, you don't," Inez emphatically agreed.

Paul and Dundas returned to the hog house and after transferring a snorting herd of hogs from an adjoining pen into the freshly cleaned lot, Dundas told Paul, "Now that one. Same as before."

"Yes, sir." Paul saluted with a grin. The combination of Dundas's odd manner and the utter lowliness of Paul's own situation had suddenly struck him as funny.

Throughout the course of the afternoon as Paul shoveled and hauled muck to the pile behind the shed, he never threw so much as a curious glance in the direction of Vanessa's lair. He'd seen enough of her for one day. What Dundas did with himself while Paul worked, Paul could not say. He knew only that Dundas would periodically appear by the pen, catch Paul's eye and nod, disappear into one building or another, then reappear again a short time later. On several occasions Paul attempted to engage Dundas in a conversation (he wanted to learn more about the man named Hennley who sometimes got out of the devil's hole), yet Dundas evidently was not in a mood for talking and Paul never got more than an "Excuse me, I'm busy" out of him.

Somehow, despite his blistered hand and sore

shoulder, Paul survived until quitting time without col-
lapsing, going crazy, or walking off the job. He was,
however, about as beat as a fifteen-year-old boy can
be when he arrived back at the house at quarter to five.

Paul hosed off his no-longer-new-looking boots and
left them to dry in the garage. He then dragged himself
up to his room, took a hot shower, and flopped down
for a much-needed snooze. Somehow he awoke in time
to get dressed and join Ada, Hargrove, and Granny Furr
in the dining room for dinner. Without Ellis at the table
the mood was less tense than the night before, and Paul
(famished after working all day) was able to concentrate
on enjoying his food.

Five minutes after the dishes had been cleared,
Paul was back upstairs, sprawled out on his bed. He
was so tired he had not bothered to undress or to be-
moan his fate before falling asleep.

On Tuesday morning, Paul was sent to work with Ellis in a recently timbered patch of land in the southeast corner of the farm. Paul had known that eventually he was bound to have to work alone with Ellis, yet that knowledge did not exempt him from dreading the assignment.

They traveled to the patch on the farm's big Allis-Chalmers tractor, behind which trailed a wagon. The timbered ground was slated to become a field. First, though, all rocks, roots, stumps, and other debris had to be removed, loaded into the wagon, and hauled away. No one expected the job to be completed

five

before autumn. The crew tackled it only when other, more important chores were done.

Ellis unhitched the wagon and parked in the middle of the cleared area, and then while he used the tractor to chain-yank stumps from the ground, Paul went around with a long crowbar, prying rocks and horizontal roots from the ground. It wasn't long before Paul decided he enjoyed clearing land more than shoveling muck. The air was fresh and clean, Ellis basically left him alone in his labors, and Paul derived a certain, simple satisfaction from digging in the dirt. Also, he had remembered that morning to borrow a pair of gloves from the supply shelf in the garage, so his hands did not suffer as they did the day before.

They slowly filled the wagon, then later that morning hauled it to a nearby gulley, into which they unloaded the refuse by hand. Paul was throwing a root over the side of the wagon when an incongruous splash of color caught his eye. The splash originated in a meadow approximately seventy yards from the gulley. Curious, Paul paused, peered into the meadow, and soon discerned a blue blouse and pink shorts. In them was a girl with long, almond-colored hair that fell midway down her back. She was standing perfectly still, apparently studying some creature or object that was obscured from Paul's view. The girl was too far away for him to determine the color of her eyes, yet he was able to guess from the shape of her body that she was fourteen or fifteen. Maybe older. Whatever her age, she did not move a muscle the whole while Paul observed her.

Ellis noticed Paul staring into the distance and wondered, "What do you see, a ghost?"

Paul was startled by Ellis's voice, as well as chagrined to be caught slacking off. "No." Paul's tone was defensive.

"What, then?" asked Ellis. "You can go ahead and tell me if you saw a ghost."

Paul looked doubtfully at Ellis. "It's not a ghost. I saw a girl. She's standing over there in the meadow."

Ellis nodded, then with no hint of irony or humor said, "There's supposed to be a ghost in the area. I was just wondering if you'd seen it."

Paul thought of Dundas's story about the deceased hired hand who sometimes got out of the devil's hole and recalled Granny's remark about him being easily spooked . . . and ventured a wild guess, "You're not talking about Hennley, are you?"

Ellis's face fell. "Where'd you hear about Hennley?"

"From Dundas."

"Hmph," Ellis huffed. "Yeah, well, maybe I was talking about Hennley. Or maybe I wasn't."

Paul was having a hard time believing what he was hearing. For all he could read in Ellis's eyes, the man was serious about what he was saying. "Look, I'll show you." Paul turned and raised a hand to point, but the meadow was empty. The girl was gone. "I, ah . . . she was there a second ago."

Ellis studied Paul, thinking Lord knows what.

"I swear," Paul blurted. "She was standing near those bushes, looking at something. I couldn't see what."

The corner of Ellis's mouth stretched upward in a smirk. "Do you often suffer delusions?"

"No, I don't suffer delusions. You're the one seeing ghosts, Ellis. I told you I saw a person, that's all."

Ellis laughed. "No need to get hot. And just for the record, I didn't say *I'd* seen a ghost. I said there was supposed to be one in the area."

Paul was beginning to perceive that Ellis might be more complex and interesting than he'd previously imagined. Still, he felt their conversation was headed in a direction where he was not currently inclined to go and bent to pick up a root, which he hurled forcefully into the gulley.

Ellis also returned to the task at hand, and after a moment informed Paul, "I suspect you saw Rebecca. She wanders a lot and is liable to turn up anywhere."

"Oh?" Paul hoped Ellis would say more about Rebecca, but the man withdrew thoughtfully into himself and proceeded to unload the wagon without saying another word. In fact, Paul did not hear Ellis speak again until just before they broke for lunch an hour later, and then all he heard was Ellis addressing an obstinate stump that provoked his ire.

Paul and Ellis returned from lunch and had been working for a couple of hours in the new field when Ellis switched off the tractor and walked over to where Paul was digging in the ground. He watched Paul labor for a moment, and then — in what seemed to Paul like an attempt to be friendly — asked in an idly curious tone, "So, what sort of trouble were you in back home?"

Paul hesitated, feigning confusion.

"You know, for being sent here."

Paul knew what Ellis was asking; he just needed a moment to compose himself. "I got caught lying," Paul finally said with a blush. "It was an innocent lie. Things just went wrong with it."

Ellis laughed. He wasn't mocking Paul. He was genuinely amused. "Those innocent lies will get you every time. What happened?"

Paul jabbed the iron bar he was holding in the ground. He accepted responsibility for what he'd done, but he wasn't proud to do so. "A guy named Stitch asked me to provide him with an alibi, to say he'd been with me one night. I had seen him briefly that evening, for about five minutes, so when a cop came and asked me about it, I sort of stretched the truth and said we'd been hanging out. The thing was, Stitch forgot to tell me he'd borrowed his uncle's car and sideswiped some woman's car, then took off because he didn't have a license."

Ellis wrinkled his brow. "That doesn't sound good."

"No," Paul grimly agreed. "It was an ugly situation. The woman didn't have any insurance and wanted to sue for damages . . . and after my name was dragged into the mess, my dad had to step in and sort things out with the judge and Stitch's uncle's insurance company."

"I guess you're lucky your dad's a lawyer," Ellis observed with a disapproving smirk.

Paul winced and looked down.

"Remember you mentioned Hennley this morning?"

Paul raised his eyes and nodded.

"He used to say, 'Taffy stretches, but not the truth.'"

Paul thought hard for several seconds. He felt like screaming at Ellis: "I'm ashamed enough already. No need to twist a knife in me!" But Paul did not scream.

Instead, he said humbly, "It seems I'm meant to learn that the hard way."

Ellis stared flatly at Paul for a moment, then sighed, gave Paul a sympathetic look, and said in a suddenly gloomy and pensive tone of voice, "Hard way or soft, we learn however we learn. Anyhow, I doubt three months of farming will kill you. At least you'll be free in September. Me, I'll be planting corn until I die."

Paul was taken aback by Ellis's abrupt change of mood. It was as if someone had reached over and flicked a switch. Sensing a need to say something, Paul asked, "Is farming so bad? Or do you have something else you'd rather do?"

Ellis pondered before replying, "No, I was born to this land. Farming suits me. My problem is, I never had much of a choice about the matter. I came home from college the day after Dad's leg was crushed and never went back. Everyone just expected me to take over."

"What happened to your dad's leg?"

"A bull went ballistic and slammed him against a tree. If Hennley hadn't of been there, Dad might've been killed."

It was Paul's turn to give Ellis a sympathetic look, and as he did, it occurred to him that he'd already done what his father had advised him not to do: rushed to judgment on the people he met.

*Perhaps Ellis wasn't an impossible person,* Paul now allowed.

"I know how it feels not to have much of a choice about matters," Paul said after a pause. "I hope you'll warn me if we see that bull."

"We won't," Ellis replied matter-of-factly. "I shot that bull myself."

Paul was a little less weary that evening than he'd been the day before, and so after supper he went out to sit on the front veranda. He'd just gotten settled when Granny Furr ambled outdoors. "You a fan of sunsets?" she inquired as she ensconced herself in a cushioned chair beside Paul.

"I guess so," he replied, not having thought one way or the other about the matter. He'd never spent time near the mountains before and did not know just how spectacular the sunsets could be. All that was about to change, for this evening in June had just the right amount of clouds carrying just the right amount

six

of moisture at the proper time of day to produce a fanfare of refracted, pastel colors. Together, he and Granny watched as a mauve-and-scarlet ribbon drifted over the solitary summit of Gallihugh Mountain and was absorbed into a larger band of orange-and-purple clouds. Paul was astounded by the show. They didn't get sunsets of this caliber in Richmond.

After a little while, Granny remarked, "It may rain tomorrow."

"Think so?" Paul didn't doubt Granny's prognosis. He was just curious.

The old woman gurgled with amusement. "I wouldn't bet the farm, but yes, I think it will be raining by morning."

Paul nodded and turned back toward the mountains. He was soon distracted by the furry tip of an upraised tail bobbing along the outside wall of the veranda. The tail approached an open set of steps, and then Einstein stepped into view. He bounded onto the veranda, walked over to Granny Furr, and nudged her knee with his nose. "There's my boy," Granny cooed and patted the dog's head. He absorbed her affections for approximately ten seconds, then turned and strode over to Paul.

Except for wincing, Paul did not move. The last time he and Einstein had been this close, the dog had nipped at his backside. A round of eye wrestling ensued, lasting until Einstein evidently decided to let bygones be bygones and humbly lowered his head. Paul knew a truce offer when he saw one and reached down to scratch the top of the dog's head. Einstein made a contented noise, and Paul asked Granny, "Did you know his owner?"

"Of course I knew Hennley Gray. The man worked here for twenty-five years."

"Oh," said Paul. To him, twenty-five years seemed

like an awful long time to do anything, much less work on anyone's farm. "What sort of man was Hennley?"

"He was the best sort of man," Granny said with simple conviction. "He was modest and he cared about his word."

"You mean he was dependable?"

"You could count on Hennley, yes," Granny told Paul, dipping her snowy white head. "But I meant that he was always cautious about what he said or did not say. Hennley respected words. I think he believed they lived in the air after they were spoken."

Paul grew suddenly self-conscious. Was Granny Furr preaching to him? Did she know why he'd been sent to the farm?

Granny noticed Paul's confusion and offered, "You know how some people talk without listening to what they say?"

Paul nodded. He knew.

"Well, that was the opposite of Hennley Gray. He had very little tolerance for prattling fools."

Paul nodded again and scratched behind the ear that Einstein presented for special attention.

A knowing smile appeared on Granny's wrinkled face. "Einstein will sit there all night if you keep scratching."

"I may do just that," said Paul. "Now that we're friends, I'm almost afraid to stop."

Granny hemmed with amusement and turned her gaze to the mountains. "You have the same coloring as Hennley Gray . . . and that dimple in your chin is almost identical to the one he had."

Paul sensed from Granny's tone of voice and manner that it was an honor to be compared with Hennley. "Dundas told me we looked alike."

"As you do," Granny confirmed.

The sun fell behind the mountains, dusk danced across the veranda, and Granny Furr rose stiffly from her chair. "I melt if I sit out at night," she said playfully. "You be well."

Paul smiled, bid Granny good night with a respectful nod, quit scratching Einstein, and sat back. More than satisfied with the treatment he had received, the dog lay contentedly at his new friend's feet.

In the following half hour Paul got so wrapped up thinking about words living in the air, about taffy stretching but not the truth, about a girl named Rebecca standing in a meadow . . . he did not notice that the stars came out and then were obscured by a dense blanket of clouds.

It was raining when Paul awoke on Wednesday morning. For him, rain was just rain — an inconvenient reason to look for his hat — but he was not a farmer with many thousands of dollars invested in seed and fertilizer. For a farmer, rain was a blessing, part of a faithful bargain made with Mother Nature. Indeed, given the choice between a withering drought or watching their crops swept away in a flood, most farmers would choose the latter option.

At the post-breakfast meeting that morning, Hargrove sent Tucker and Ellis with Dundas to the hog house with instructions to select and deliver a dozen prime-weight hogs to the weekly farm auction in Fenton. Hargrove then asked Paul if he had any objections to helping Ada with some chores around the house, and Paul, of course, said he did not.

Paul spent the first half of the day painting shelves in the garage, then after lunch he helped Ada sort through years of accrued clutter in the basement. Most of what they found was junk, which Paul hauled up the steps and threw in the back of the green farm truck. Each time he went to the truck he said hello to Einstein, who spent a dry afternoon lying beneath the vehicle.

About half an hour before quitting time Paul

returned to the basement, where he found Ada sitting cross-legged on the floor, looking through a box of photographs. A lock of dark hair had escaped from her bun and dangled loosely in front of her nose. She did not look up or give any sign of noticing Paul's entrance into the room, so he stopped in the doorway and quietly watched her studying the photograph she held in her hand. She was smiling, and Paul thought of how pretty she must have been when she was younger. It was an innocent thought, one of those whimsical conjectures a wandering mind makes on a rainy day.

Ada startled Paul by laughing, then surprised him further by speaking as if she'd been aware of his presence all along. "Come here, Paul," she said without looking up. "You might get a kick out of this."

The picture Ada handed Paul was of a teenage Ellis dressed in a black-and-white tuxedo. Beside him was a lanky girl in a cherry-red dress. An inch or two taller than Ellis, she had a thick mane of striking, pumpkin-colored hair.

"Ellis is sixteen there," said Ada. "That's before his junior–senior prom. It was Ellis and Maya's first date."

Paul was intrigued by the image of Ellis without a beard. There was an element of gentle sensitivity in the younger Ellis's face that was no longer readily apparent in the man. When Paul handed the picture back to Ada, she glanced at it wistfully and said, "It's a peculiar passage when a mother watches her son fall in love."

*63*

"He did? With Maya?"

"Yes, madly. And she with him, I think. She lives in Charlottesville now, teaches the third grade, but she's been spending a lot of her summer vacation here on the farm. Hargrove and I have been waiting for them to get married."

"I worked with Ellis yesterday. He never mentioned a girlfriend."

Ada huffed and placed the photograph back in the box. "Ellis wouldn't mention a tornado unless it blew away his house and he needed a place to sleep."

After Paul hauled the last load of junk up from the basement and threw it in the back of the old pickup truck, he stood for a while in the drizzling rain, looking over Ellis's house in the valley. Einstein soon crawled out from under the truck and stood beside him. "Hey there, fellow," Paul greeted the dog. "I understand you miss your master."

To Paul's astonishment, Einstein made a guttural noise and nodded affirmatively.

"You understand English, do you?"

Again, Einstein nodded.

Or maybe Paul just imagined that he nodded. It didn't really matter. Paul wanted to talk and Einstein was there to listen.

"Maybe you can tell me, what am I supposed to

think? My dad said the Vallenports lived in the real world, yet he never mentioned that world included a grown man that refuses to drive, a six-hundred-pound lovelorn sow, a ghost that climbs in and out of the devil's hole, and words that live in the air."

Paul looked at Einstein, who rested his brown eyes attentively on Paul, but did not say a word. Paul shrugged, and before turning to go inside, told Einstein, "Maybe Dad didn't know."

Paul did not ride in the green farm truck until Friday morning. Tucker Dyson was driving. They were headed to the barn lot beside Ellis's house to get the tractor and the tools they would need for refurbishing a fence at a place called "the upper field." It was less than a mile from the big house to the barn, yet plenty far for Paul to experience a bird's-eye view of Einstein's truck-blocking tactics. The fearless dog drew so close to the tire on several of his mad charges that Paul cringed and braced for a collision. Fortunately, one never occurred.

Unfortunately, however, Paul was a step too slow

*seven*

with the gate at the foot of the hill and Einstein flashed through before he could slam it closed. "Sorry," Paul apologized to Tucker as he hopped back into the cab of the truck.

Tucker wasn't bothered. "Not your fault. Einstein makes it about thirty percent of the time."

As the truck, blocked by Einstein and hemmed in by ditches on either side of the road, crept along at approximately twelve miles per hour, Paul asked Tucker, "Do you ever let Einstein ride?"

"Sometimes." Tucker smiled thinly. "Only problem is, once he's in, you need a winch to get him out."

Tucker parked in front of Ellis's house and told Paul to fetch the wire stretcher from the toolroom in the barn while he got the tractor and other supplies they would need.

Paul hesitated before departing on his errand. Although he was slightly embarrassed to do so, he had to ask, "What's a wire stretcher look like?"

Tucker replied as if it was a perfectly legitimate question, "It's shorter than a baseball bat and has a chain attached to one end."

Paul nodded and hurried off. It took him several minutes to find the toolroom and the wire stretcher, and when he exited the barn and started toward the front lot he saw Tucker reclining in the seat of the small Ford tractor. The man had one booted foot propped against the steering wheel, the other leg slung over the left tire, and he was gazing intently at the singular peak of Gallihugh Mountain.

Paul slowed his pace and studied Tucker as he approached him. Somewhere in his mid-forties, Tucker had a chiseled face and amazingly bright blue eyes. He was (as Hargrove had introduced him) a handsome gent, and there was something about his demeanor that elicited deep respect from Paul.

Paul was less than ten yards from the tractor when

the old rooster that no one could catch began to crow. It was hidden in a copse of trees between Ellis's house and the barn. Tucker emerged from his reverie and looked toward the trees. When he did he saw Paul, whom he studied for an instant before saying, "It was about a year ago that Hennley Gray hung himself in the barn."

Paul was taken aback by the news. Neither Dundas nor Granny nor Ellis had said anything about a hanging.

Paul looked down. He could not help but wonder if his resemblance to the deceased man had stirred Tucker's memory.

"Of course, you never knew Hennley."

Paul looked up. "I've heard him mentioned. Dundas said Einstein was Hennley's dog, and the green truck belonged to Hennley as well."

"True," said Tucker, and after gazing solemnly at Paul for several seconds, he shifted in the tractor seat and reached for the ignition. "Come on. Wedge that wire stretcher next to the fender here and hop on the rear hitch."

Paul did as he was bid, and with Einstein watching from under the truck, Tucker drove from the barn lot. They followed a narrow, tree-lined lane that wound its way into the hills on the west side of the farm, turned onto a trail that ran through a pasture occupied by tail-swishing, Black Angus cattle, and headed up a long slope toward the upper field.

Tucker parked in the shade of a giant oak and they went to work on the fence. While Tucker stripped all sagging and broken wire from the locust posts, Paul gathered the discarded strands and put them into piles for later collection. The barbed wire was rusty and stiff, and it wasn't long before Paul had more nicks and scratches on his arms and hands than he cared to count.

They worked their way around the field in just under two hours, then Tucker declared it was time for a break and went to the tractor, where he retrieved a thermos and paper cups from under the seat. Afterward, he sat in the shade of the oak tree and filled two cups with ice tea. Paul settled on the ground a few feet from Tucker, accepted the cup he was handed, and drained it in one long, thirsty gulp.

Tucker grinned. "Careful you don't drown."

"Yes, sir."

Tucker gestured at the thermos. "Help yourself to more if you want, but quit with the sir stuff. It makes me nervous."

Paul nodded and refilled his cup. He took a moderate sip, was silent for a spell, then asked Tucker, "What you said about Hennley Gray in the barn — why'd he do that?"

Tucker's expression went flat, and he did not

speak or move for almost a minute. Whatever he was thinking, it was tainted with anguish, and Paul felt a pang of regret for having asked the question.

Finally, somberly, Tucker said, "Hennley was already dying before he strung up the rope. I didn't know it then — he never said a word — but a cancer had been eating his stomach for months. It sure threw me. He was my friend. We worked together every day and I never suspected he was ill."

Paul waited a bit before asking, "How did you find out?"

"Mrs. Vallenport. Hennley and Ada, they talked a lot. She claims he made her swear not to tell us."

It was apparent that he held Hennley's memory in high regard. Tucker crumpled the empty cup in his hand.

Paul was intrigued. The more he learned about the man who looked like him, the more he wanted to know.

"You asked why Hennley did what he did. I've asked that often myself. He was a proud individual. I think he hung himself so no one would have to take care of him near the end." Tucker sighed and got to his feet. "Grab a hammer and pouch of staples from the toolbox. I'll show you how to stretch barbed wire."

Paul drained his cup and stood. He could feel Tucker's sadness over the loss of his friend and vicariously shared a dose of that sorrow.

Some seventy minutes later when the lunch horn sounded, Paul knew how to wield a wire stretcher. He wasn't particularly fast or efficient with the tool, yet he could perform the task, and the strands of wire he had stretched were now hammered permanently in place. Paul was personally proud of his new skill. Whereas anyone could shovel muck or pry roots from the ground, he figured pulling barbed wire took real farming know-how.

Paul and Tucker returned from lunch and finished the upper field by a quarter to four. "What do you say we sit a spell?" Tucker asked after they were done.

Paul thought that was a terrific idea and plopped down under the oak tree before Tucker could bend his knees. They enjoyed the view for a while, then Paul tentatively inquired, "Tucker, could you clear up something for me?"

"If I can."

"The first day I worked with Dundas, he told me that Einstein had belonged to Hennley Gray, and then he told me that Hennley was down in the hole with the devil, but sometimes got out. That's, ah . . . well, I'm not sure what Dundas meant."

Tucker smiled and shook his head. "Dundas is a peculiar bird. Hennley used to say he was the original, original thinker."

Tucker paused thoughtfully before continuing.

"I've heard Dundas say that about Hennley being in the devil's hole. Fact is, Hennley was cremated. I spread his ashes myself . . . some of them in the field yonder. Anyhow, Dundas didn't like the idea. He says cremation is a sin. I think his story about Hennley and the devil's hole is his way of denying what he doesn't want to accept."

Paul gazed receptively at Tucker.

"Dundas has another strange story he tells now about Hennley."

"Oh? What?"

"Well." Tucker sounded dubious. "According to Dundas, he's seen a ghost that's a dead ringer for Hennley. Pardon the pun. Those are his words, not mine. Anyhow, he says he's seen it several times. He told me that he and the ghost took a long walk one evening."

Paul had already heard of the possibility of a ghost

on the farm, so he wasn't shocked by what Tucker told him. Still, it was unsettling to hear the phantasmagorical fact stated so plainly.

"I think of Hennley every day," Tucker continued. "Sometimes I get an eerie feeling that he's watching me . . . so maybe his ghost is hovering around here. Before I believe that, though, I'd have to see it. And if I did, I'd still have to consider what I saw."

Paul gave Tucker an ambiguous look and nodded. If the man had not been sitting next to Paul with a look of seriousness in his eye, Paul might have dismissed the whole matter as unfounded nonsense. But Tucker was sitting there, and Paul could only wonder what he himself might believe or disbelieve if he actually saw a ghost.

Paul slept late on Saturday, his body hungry for the rest after five days of physical activity. It was ten-fifteen when he opened his eyes. The first thing he did was look at the wad of twenty-dollar bills on the table by his bed. There were eight altogether, representing one week's wages. He'd been suprised when Hargrove handed him the money. No one had mentioned his being paid for his labors, and Paul had never thought to ask. He didn't argue, though. In his mind the money lifted him from the status of an indentured servant and established him as a hired hand.

Paul lingered in bed, wondering what to do with

*eight*

the day. He regretted not having his computer on the farm, but he didn't own a laptop and packing and transporting his cumbersome desktop had not seemed practical. Hmm. Paul considered his options. Then it hit him: *I'll climb Gallihugh Mountain*.

He slipped out of bed, got dressed, and went down to the kitchen, where he'd been told by Inez to fend for himself. (She did not work weekends.) He poured cereal in a bowl and opened the refrigerator for milk. The first thing he saw was a platter with a note that read: DEAR BEANPOLE. KEEP WITH THE PROGRAM. The platter was heaped with fried chicken, ham sandwiches, and corn pudding in paper cups. Paul grinned. Inez Buttons was working her way into his heart.

He was washing his bowl when he saw Ada in the flower bed outside the kitchen window. He went to say good morning and ask if Gallihugh Mountain was open to the public.

"You're free to go up there," she replied, then volunteered directions on the best route for him to follow. Afterward she added, "Your mother called this morning. I told her you were well — which I hope you are — and I said you'd call her back."

"Thanks, I am well, and I'll call her," Paul replied, reaching to scratch Einstein, who had walked over to nudge his thigh. Out of the corner of his eye, Paul saw Ada studying him closely and he wondered if she was thinking that he looked like Hennley.

Whatever she was thinking, she said, "You two seem to get along. See if he'll follow you up the mountain. It might do that rascal some good to be away from the truck for a few hours."

Paul agreed to take Einstein, and after returning to the kitchen and putting a bottle of water and a couple of sandwiches in a bag (one for him and one for his four-legged friend), he exited through the garage, and he and Einstein started down the hill.

They were turning at the fork below the gate when

Paul glanced into the valley and saw Ellis sitting on his front porch steps beside a woman. Paul recognized the unusual color of the woman's hair, remembered that her name was Maya, and wondered what sort of person she might be.

Paul and Einstein proceeded past the turnoff to the upper field and continued by the fastidiously maintained ranch house that belonged to Dundas Shoals. Paul thought Dundas was an interesting person and did not mind working with the man in the hog house, but he had no inclination to voluntarily visit Dundas at home — especially not after hearing that he claimed to have taken an evening stroll with Hennley Gray's ghost.

Paul and Einstein passed under the boughs of the twin elm trees that Ada had mentioned and continued along a scantly used dirt road running west along the hump of a ridge. Straight ahead was Gallihugh Mountain.

There was nary a cloud in the sky and the late morning sun made Paul grateful he'd worn a cap. As he and Einstein journeyed west, Einstein wandered on and off the old road, investigating smells and other possibilities in the scrub brush growing on either side of the ridge.

Paul also wandered, although he did so mentally, and his thoughts eventually led him back to Richmond and the friends he was missing. He was dwelling on them and the unfortunate event that precipitated his isolation when Einstein reappeared on the road. "Hey," Paul said warmly, then continued in a confiding tone, "I've been missing my people. I bet the gang is hanging at the mall right now . . . or lounging around Judy Spelaza's pool. Now there's a girl who knows how to wear a bikini. I doubt you'd like her, though. She's got this yappy little poodle that behaves worse than a prissy cat. But Franklin Greene, he's your kind of guy. He's always peeing in the bushes."

Paul suddenly stopped talking. Einstein's head was cocked to one side and he was watching Paul with what appeared to be a worried expression. It occurred to Paul that maybe Hennley used to speak to Einstein in a similar manner, and that maybe Paul was confusing the poor creature.

He pulled the water bottle from the bag he was carrying and drank. He was about to offer a sip to Einstein when the dog turned and trotted off in the direction they had been heading.

The top of the ridge grew more narrow and the slopes steeper as Paul drew closer to Gallihugh Mountain. He began to look for the cottage Ada had told him he would see on his left. He recalled her words. "You'll come to a gate with a swale below it. Across the way you'll see a cream-colored cottage." Paul remembered that at this point a faraway look had entered Ada's eyes and her voice had fallen into a lower register. "It's a shame, really. The place has been empty now for a year. Anyhow, fifty yards or so beyond the gate, still on your left, you'll find a trail leading up the mountain."

Paul saw a gate and walked over to get a better view of the cottage. He was startled by what he saw: In the front yard, sitting on a wooden bench, was the girl from the meadow — Rebecca. Her legs were crossed at the ankles, her arms were stretched along the back of the bench, and she was basking her face in the sun. A lawn mower was parked in the yard and approximately half of the grass had been recently cut. A door to a metal shed beside the cottage stood open.

Paul didn't feel exactly right watching Rebecca without her being aware of his presense, yet he was not immediately willing to tear his eyes away and proceed up the mountain. He wanted to study her a while longer. Then he would slip away. At least that was his plan before Einstein barked, slipped under the gate, and ran down into the swale, heading for the cottage.

Rebecca had turned at the barking sound and now stared directly at Paul. After a second or two, she raised a hand and waved.

Paul felt his right hand rise of its own volition and rock from side to side.

As he read the situation, he had three viable options. He could stand there waving forever, continue up the mountain, or cross the swale and introduce himself. Although it took him nearly a minute to decide, he chose the option that made his heart beat faster.

A weed-ridden driveway delivered Paul into the low ground between the gate and the cottage, where he was temporarily out of Rebecca's line of sight. He halted by a honeysuckle vine, plucked a trumpet-shaped flower, bit away the pedicel, and drank the sweet nectar. Paul was puzzled by Rebecca's presence at the cottage. Yes, Ellis had said she was liable to turn up anywhere, yet he clearly remembered Ada telling him the place was empty. Rebecca had apparently been mowing the front lawn of the cottage. Why?

Einstein was sitting in the yard next to the bench when Paul ascended the far slope and approached

nine

along a fieldstone walkway. Rebecca watched him alertly, yet calmly. She was wearing cutoff blue jeans and a sand-colored shirt a shade lighter than her hair. Paul could see now that her eyes were brilliantly blue, and although the expression on her face was presently beset with seriousness and the bridge of her narrow nose was a little crooked, he thought she was beautiful. "Hi. I saw you here. I'm Paul."

"I know." Some of the seriousness left her face. "You work for the Vallenports."

"How'd you know that?"

"My dad told me," Rebecca replied, reaching down to scratch Einstein on the head. She asked the dog, "What are you doing so far from your truck? Have you made a new friend?"

Einstein glanced at Paul, returned his gaze to Rebecca, and wagged his tail.

"Who's your dad?"

"Tucker Dyson." Rebecca sat back and added, "He said you were very helpful."

Paul blushed, both with modesty and because he had not immediately noticed what was now so obvious: Of course Rebecca was Tucker's daughter. They had similarly shaped, squarish chins and her eyes were his, only bluer and more luminescent. "You're Rebecca, right? Ellis told me. I saw you standing in a meadow this week."

"On Tuesday." Rebecca smiled. She had a reserved manner, yet was not shy. "I saw you looking at me."

Until now, Paul had felt relatively composed. However, in the quicksilver turn of an instant he lost access to his own good senses and could not find a stable thought in his head. He'd known pretty girls before (even kissed one once), yet he'd never met anyone who made him feel as transparent as he felt now.

Disconcerted by the feeling that she was looking through him, Paul gazed around the yard, feigning interest in the quality of the grass. The mower caught his eye and he was struck by a notion. He stepped forward and set the paper bag he'd been carrying on the bench beside Rebecca. "Seeing as I have a reputation for being helpful, I'll cut the rest of the yard for you."

A small noise escaped from Rebecca. It suggested that she'd been tickled.

"What's so funny?"

Rebecca suppressed her amusement and stood. "I'm quite capable of finishing the lawn, Paul."

"I'm sure you are, but that's not why I offered." Paul strode toward the mower, grabbed the ignition cord, and before starting the engine, fatuously explained, "I love cutting grass. It's fun."

Rebecca rolled her blue-blue eyes, sat back down on the bench, and studied Paul with ambivalence. Einstein popped onto all fours at the loud sound of the mower, glared unhappily at Paul for a moment, then trotted from the yard.

As Paul pushed the mower around and around the yard, he did not even try to guess what sort of impression he was making on Rebecca. He just nodded gallantly each time he passed by the bench, then held his head up high and concentrated on cutting the grass.

Paul pushed the mower into the shed when he was done. Rebecca came over to lock the metal door, and awarded him a warm smile. "Thanks so much for your help," she said sincerely. "I'd love to sit and talk, but I promised Mom I'd be home by noon. I have to watch my little sister while Mom goes shopping."

Paul had not been harboring any precise expectations about what would happen when he finished cutting the grass, so it would be unfair to say he was crushed by Rebecca's news. However, he was visibly let down. He gamely tried to hide his disappointment with a question, although not a particularly astute one. "You have a sister?"

"Yes." Rebecca smiled. "Catherine. She's five."

"Oh," said Paul, his mind gone suddenly blank. At least it wasn't racing anymore.

Rebecca touched him lightly on the arm and turned to go. "Thanks again. I genuinely appreciate your help."

"Yeah. Sure." Paul was stuck in his tracks for a moment. Then he scrambled to grab his snack bag and catch up with Rebecca. "I'm headed up the mountain. I'll walk you to the gate."

Rebecca didn't reply audibly, yet said with her eyes that she approved. Paul was glad and carefully maintained a respectful distance between them as they walked. He was afraid she already thought he was nuts and didn't want her thinking he was pushy as well. When they reached the honeysuckle vine in the lowland, Paul plucked a flower and said, "These taste great, you know. Ever had one?"

Although Rebecca's responding look was not quite cutting, it was sharp. "I did grow up on a farm, Paul."

"Sorry," Paul muttered, not trying or even hoping to hide his embarrassment.

Rebecca kindly noted, "I'm sure you don't find much honeysuckle where you're from."

"Richmond," Paul offered.

Rebecca nodded as if to imply that she already knew where Paul lived.

He wondered if it mattered to her that he'd been raised as a city boy, but did not inquire. He was wondering so many things at this moment, he could hardly separate them in his mind. Finally, as they drew close to the gate, one of Paul's wonderings took precedent over the others and he asked, "Whose yard did we just cut?"

He could almost see the question hit Rebecca. The skin around her eyes drew taut and her whole mood shifted, or rather sank. Paul lifted the wooden latch and swung the gate open. Then Rebecca said, "It's my yard, I suppose. The person that lived there died last year and left the place to me."

Paul held the gate for Rebecca. He had a hunch as to the name of the deceased. "Hennley Gray?"

Rebecca stopped suddenly, eyeing Paul with a mixture of solemnity and surprise. "Yes," she said after collecting herself and continuing through the gate. "That was Hennley's cottage. How did you know?"

Paul followed, closing the gate behind him. "I didn't know. I guessed. But Hennley's name has come up more than a few times this week, and from what I can tell, he's sorely missed."

"'Sorely missed' is one way of putting it," Rebecca told Paul in a sorrowful voice. "It seems to me, there's been a hole in the world since Hennley went away."

Paul lowered his eyes respectfully.

"Dad told me that you looked like Hennley."

"Do I?"

"Some. Enough to look twice. But Hennley was so much his own self. There was only one him."

Paul nodded. He understood. And when Rebecca extended her right hand, he shook it.

"I have to go now," she said. "I'm sure we'll meet again soon."

"Hope so," said Paul, watching as Rebecca turned and walked away. It was not until after she disappeared that he thought of Einstein and wondered where he'd gone.

Paul was so preoccupied with half-formed thoughts and inarticulate emotions that he hardly noticed his surroundings as he trudged up the steep slope of Gallihugh Mountain. It wasn't until he gained the summit and followed the footpath to a lookout rock that he returned fully to the here and now. The view from the rock was majestic. Rolling out below him like a green-and-brown patchwork quilt lay the broad sweep of the Vallenports' farm, and beyond. As he admired the view he was visited by a strange thought — the kind of thought that might be found only on a mountaintop. It took the form of a question: *What if I was sent here to remind people of Hennley Gray so I could learn about his life?*

As Paul chewed on the question, a subset of smaller questions came into his mind: *Learn what? That words live in the air? That the truth is not taffy?*

Paul shook off these questions and was soon visited by another mountaintop thought: *There lies the entirety of the quiet, self-contained little world where Rebecca Dyson lives and where a hole has been punctured.*

Paul had hardly finished receiving this thought when he was distracted by a sound on the path behind him. He turned and saw Einstein, who ambled out onto the rock and sat down.

"Hey, fellow. Good to see you," Paul said joyfully. Then he reached into the snack bag and asked, "Want a ham sandwich?"

Evidently, from Einstein's response, he wanted two.

When Paul finally got out of bed and dressed on Sunday morning the house was empty. He had declined the Vallenports' invitation to attend church with them and Granny. He went down to the kitchen and ate a bowl of cereal, then took advantage of the private time to return his mother's call. Their conversation was short and sweet, so to speak, and the one with his father was even shorter.

Way in the back of his mind, Paul knew he would eventually forgive his parents for banishing him, but that was eventually. For now, he wanted them stewing

**ten**

in the remorse he presumed they were presently feeling.

Little did Paul know that Louise and Morris Shackleford had spent the past week enjoying a second honeymoon of sorts, and although aware of their son's absence, had not experienced an iota of remorse.

After hanging up the phone, Paul decided to take a stroll around the farm. The night before, at dinner, he had asked Hargrove where Tucker lived, and was told, "Below that cleared patch where you and Ellis were working the other day is a little dirt road that runs between the woods and the cornfield. He lives back in there. Why, you planning to pay Tucker a visit?"

"No, sir. Just wondering where he lives," Paul had answered, then spent the next several hours agonizing over his disingenuous response. Technically, what he'd told Hargrove was true — he had no plans to visit Tucker at home. Still, by failing to mention his interest in Rebecca he had withheld a portion of the truth. It was a small infraction. Even so, after what he'd been through and the promise he'd made to himself and his father, he was disappointed with his less-than-fully-honest reply.

*It probably was not,* Paul later reflected, *the way Hennley Gray would have answered Hargrove.*

When Paul exited through the garage he saw Einstein lying under the truck. He had his head on his front paws and was wearing a droopy expression. "What's the matter?"

Einstein raised an eyebrow, then let it drop.

"Want to go for a walk?"

Einstein showed no response.

Paul went to the truck, squatted down, and gave Einstein a good scratch. "It's okay, boy. Sometimes I get lonely too. I know you miss Hennley . . . you'll get over that. I hope. Now come on. Let's go for a walk."

Einstein did not move. He wasn't in the mood for a walk.

"Fine," said Paul. "Stay put if you want."

He left the dog under the truck, ambled down the front hill, and let his spirit guide him where it would. No surprise, he found himself standing in a bend on the dirt road between the cornfield and the woods where the new field was being cleared. Through a gap in the trees he saw the roofline of a house. He did not approach the house. He just stood for a minute or two, then turned around and walked to the gulley where he and Ellis had dumped the wagonload of debris and where he had first seen Rebecca Dyson.

He sat for an hour, imagining all the fun his friends were having back home in Richmond and regretting the small, innocent lie that put him here on the lip of a refuse-strewn gulley. Of course, it was now emphatically obvious to him that "small" and "innocent" did not apply to lying. The one he had uttered had grown into a guilty monster soon after he released it into the air. *Or at least,* Paul thought, *that's how Hennley might have explained the situation.*

Paul suddenly caught himself and shifted mental gears: *What am I doing . . . thinking about what a dead man I've never met might say? Next thing I know I'll be believing in ghosts and looking down in holes for the devil.*

Paul was walking on the paved road that ran through the valley below the big house when he was startled by the sound of his own name. He turned and saw Ellis standing on his front porch. Maya was in the shadows behind him. Ellis waved and called to Paul, "Come here. I want to introduce you to someone."

Paul crossed to the house, and as he stepped onto the porch Maya stepped forward to shake his hand. Paul barely heard Ellis saying each of their names. The forefront of his consciousness was busy registering Maya's charismatic presense. For one thing, she was almost six feet tall. For another, a stream of sunlight was reflecting brightly off her pumpkin-colored hair and made it seem that her head was afire. Lastly, her large, greenish eyes were nearly translucent.

"So you're Paul," Maya observed with friendly aplomb.

"Yes," Paul nodded and did a pretty good job of hiding his discomfiture. Maya's beaded necklace and the multicolored, loose-fitting dress she was wearing reminded him of a hippie from the sixties.

"Pleased to meet you." Maya released Paul's hand. "I hear you are fitting in well on the farm."

Paul shrugged. "I hope so, if that's what you heard."

Maya flashed a white-toothed smile. "That's what I heard. When is your birthday, Paul?"

"October."

"What day?" Maya wondered, and after Paul told her, she observed under her breath: "A Libra. Hmm. How interesting."

Paul glanced at Ellis and saw that he was mildly amused by something. There was an awkward pause (awkward for Paul, not for Ellis and Maya), and then Ellis asked, "Would you like some coffee? Or a soda?"

Paul politely declined the offer, and then after telling Maya he was glad to have made her acquaintance and nodding good-bye to Ellis, he stepped off the porch and started across the yard. He didn't turn when he heard Maya speak to Ellis, but he was pretty certain he heard her say, "You and Rebecca were right. He does remind one of Hennley."

Paul pondered those words all the way back to the big house.

*When had Maya and Rebecca spoken? Were they close friends? What else had they said about me?*

Ada, still in her Sunday best, was standing at the kitchen counter drinking hot tea when Paul entered the room. They greeted each other, and he sat on the stool beside her. Paul remembered Tucker telling him that Mrs. Vallenport and Hennley had talked a lot, and shared the secret of Hennley's illness, and Paul now saw a chance to learn more about the man.

"Since I got here I've been hearing about Hennley Gray. I know what happened to him and all. He must have been a pretty good person."

While Paul was speaking, Ada's eyes had widened with a dash of surprise, or dismay, or some wary emotion. But then her expression softened into a smile and she replied, "He was a very good person."

"Everyone says so," Paul observed. Then he offered, "I met Rebecca Dyson yesterday on my way up Gallihugh Mountain.'"

"Oh? Nice girl."

Paul nodded. "She was at the cottage. She told me Hennley left it to her. She didn't blurt it out. I asked."

Ada's smile disappeared. As she looked at Paul, he could feel the seriousness of the moment. "He had that planned beforehand. Hargrove got a package in the mail the day after he was found. Hennley had paid his taxes in advance and arranged with a lawyer for the deed to go in Rebecca's name." Ada sighed dolorously before adding, "He left us lacking when he went."

"Lacking? How do you mean?"

Ada took a sip of tea and considered for a moment before replying. "It's not the loss that's hard to live with. One gets over that shock. It's the lack of Hennley that's so hard for everyone. He had a respectful way of listening when people spoke. It's not easy to describe, but the attention he gave people made them feel as if what they were saying was important, and by extension, they were important to Hennley. Now that he's gone from the farm . . . well, there's no one to remind us every day of how important we are. That's what we lack. That and the simple honor of sharing our lives with his rare character."

Paul and Ada sat in silence for several seconds.

Then Paul cleared the air with a polite cough and asked, "What was rare about his character?"

Ada took a last sip of tea from her cup and stood before replying, "Hennley had the integrity of a tree. He was straight up and strong. Now, if you'll excuse me, it's time I changed out of this dress."

Paul watched the kitchen door swing slowly to a close behind Ada and sat, pondering the distinction she had made between the loss and the lack of a loved one. Although Paul had never suffered the loss of someone close, he sensed that Ada had been attempting to share a painfully gained insight, and he felt he owed her the effort to fully grasp her meaning. He was struggling to comprehend when he recalled overhearing Maya say to Ellis, "He does remind one of Hennley."

Maya's words caused Paul to wonder: *Is my presence disturbing people on the farm? Am I stirring up memories that should be asleep?*

Paul began his second week on the Vallenports' farm with a starkly different attitude than his first. He was still a long way from thanking Morris for sending him to the country, but he had more or less accepted his fate. In fact, he was finding the farm and the stories it had to tell far more interesting than he would have previously allowed himself to imagine. Also, thanks to Einstein, he found himself being accepted by the crew in a way that surprised him.

On Monday morning both Ellis and Tucker said that they'd heard about Paul's long walk with Einstein

eleven

on Saturday, and each had made it clear that they were impressed. Ellis had even joked, "Maybe you are a cousin of mine, although we're pretty distant, so don't let it go to your head."

The evening of that same Monday, Paul began what was to become a new habit for him: taking long, circuitious strolls around the farm each evening after work. Einstein accompanied him now and then, but only when he felt the desire, and even when he did follow along, he would sometimes abandon Paul abruptly and rush back to his beloved truck.

Paul enjoyed the relaxing mental and physical benefits of his daily strolls as much as any healthy person might, but he had no illusions about why he had adopted the routine. How else might he chance upon Rebecca Dyson? The last thing she had told him was "I'm sure we'll meet again soon." He was making himself available for that to happen.

★  ★  ★  ★  ★

On Thursday, Dundas strolled into the kitchen as lunch was being served and announced with all the pride and joy of a delighted father, "Vanessa brought a farrow of seven into the world this morning. Every one of them is squealing with health."

"Congratulations, Dundas," said Ellis.

"How's the mother?" Tucker asked solicitously.

His face suddenly growing serious, Dundas replied. "She's weary, of course, but otherwise fine . . . for her age."

Paul and Inez exchanged clandestine grins, and after the men filled their plates and exited into the nook, she quipped, "Dundas has a good heart, but sometimes I think he cares more about pigs than people."

"That could be," Paul allowed, thinking there was more truth than not to what Inez said.

That sentiment was confirmed for Paul the next day when he helped Dundas paint the cinder-block storage building at the hog house. They painted the building fire-engine red and the door a bright yellow. "The place was due for a cheering up," Dundas told Paul when he wondered about the colors. "Can't have my hogs getting depressed, can I?"

"No, sir."

They later went to view Vanessa's litter, and although Paul was reluctant to poke his head very far into the shed, he could see that the piglets were as cute as creatures could be. He remarked on their beauty to Dundas, who smiled as if personally flattered. Then Paul found the nerve to ask, "Have you really seen Hennley Gray's ghost?"

Dundas shot Paul a look that made him regret he'd ever considered posing the question. Whether Dundas had detected a hint of disrespect in Paul's voice, or disbelief, or cynicism, or whatever, he stared at Paul with a burning gaze that seemed to inquire: *Why should I satisfy the curiosity of a doubting city boy like you?*

Paul winced and stepped backward. Dundas then

turned away and there was no further discussion of the matter.

However, the look that Paul had seen in Dundas's eyes did lead Paul, for the first time since hearing the rumor, to consider the possibility that a ghost actually existed on the Vallenports' farm.

Was he spooked?

Naw. Not much. Hardly at all.

Just barely enough to tremble.

At ten-thirty on Saturday morning Paul was walking rather conspicuously back and forth along the valley road when he finally saw Rebecca. Unfortunately, it was a fleeting sight, for she was riding in a car with her mother and little sister. Although Paul was not pleased to see them heading away from the farm in the direction of town, the enthusiastic wave Rebecca extended from her window kept him from being wholly disappointed.

Each day in the following workweek was

inordinately hot and muggy, and four out of five of them ended in booming, late afternoon thundershowers. The rain was more than welcome on the farm . . . yet the storms frustrated and discouraged Paul from taking his evening strolls. Finally, on Thursday, despite an ominous bank of cumulonimbus clouds gathering in the western sky, he suppressed his better judgment and set out after dinner on a long hike.

His journey took him to the gate on the ridge road, where he stood a few moments studying Hennley's old cottage. He had turned and started for home when a sudden wind kicked up and a crackle of lightning tore across the sky above his head. He began to run, but could not outrace the storm, and was soon caught in a heavy downpour. Running seemed futile, so Paul stopped on the road and resigned himself to experiencing the elements.

As the wind whirred past him and he was pelted by the rain, Paul thought he heard a voice whisper his name. He turned and looked around. There was no one. Again, he heard his name whispered, and the voice said, "Are you leaving too?"

Startled and confused, Paul cried out, "What?"

He waited and listened.

Several moments passed, then, as quickly as it had arrived, the storm dissipated and the sky above Paul was clear. *The voice must have been a trick of the wind,* Paul told himself. *It had to be.*

*"Leaving too?" What could that mean?*

Finally, on the Saturday after seeing her in the car, on the same day he was scheduled to later depart for Richmond by bus, Paul got the chance to speak with Rebecca.

He found her sitting beside Maya on the rail fence between the barnyard and Ellis's house. Rebecca dropped from the fence and waved, and he went over to say hello. Maya, in her paisley pants and V-necked jersey, did not move from her perch.

"Hi," Rebecca said warmly and extended her hand.

Paul shook the hand and said, "Hello." His voice was just a little tight with nervousness.

"I was wondering when I'd see you again," Rebecca offered blithely.

*You were wondering!?* thought Paul, but he said, "It was bound to happen eventually."

Rebecca turned and gestured. "You know Maya?"

"We've met." Paul nodded. "Hello."

"Hi, Paul." Maya smiled. She was excessively calm and collected, and Paul thought she probably learned that from teaching third-graders.

"We were discussing the subconscious mind," volunteered Rebecca.

"You were?" Paul muttered, suddenly recalling the voice he'd heard in the storm on Thursday. Had *it* been produced by his subconscious?

"It's a matter of great interest to Maya," Rebecca answered. "She's an expert on subconsciousness."

"I wouldn't say that," Maya interjected modestly.

"You didn't. I did," Rebecca retorted.

Maya conceded to Rebecca with a dip of her head. "Even so, a little knowledge on a complex subject does not an expert make."

It was clear now to Paul that Rebecca and Maya were close friends. He also noted that Rebecca had a feisty side.

Not wanting Paul to feel left out, Rebecca considerately tried to explain. "We were talking about memory and how it's connected to changing emotions. Maya has a theory that people constantly reshape the past to fit their needs in the present."

"You mean like revisionist history?" asked Paul, pleased that he'd thought of something intelligent to say.

"Exactly," replied Maya. "And revising the present as well."

Paul hemmed and thought, *Like exaggerating and embellishing the truth . . . like lying?*

"But enough of that," Maya declared. "We were just blabbing. What are you up to, Paul?"

"Out for a walk before I leave. Actually I have to go soon. I'm catching a bus home at two-thirty."

Rebecca was surprised and noticeably concerned. "You're going home?"

"Just for the Fourth."

"So you'll be back."

"Yes, on Wednesday," Paul said quickly, realizing as he spoke that his decision about whether to return had just been made. "We're supposed to bale hay next week. The men are counting on me to help."

"Good," chimed Rebecca. "Maybe we can catch up with each other then, have that talk we didn't have before."

"Sure. I'll look forward to that," said Paul, and a moment or two later, after leaving Rebecca and Maya in the yard and starting up the hill to the big house, he was already looking forward.

Paul enjoyed his visit home. It was good to be surrounded by friends again, and he had fun gathering with the gang on the bank of James River to watch the big fireworks show. And yet, there was something not quite fulfulling about his return. For one thing, it was clear to him that his friends were only superficially interested in his experiences on the farm. They gladly welcomed Paul back into their world, but were simply not curious about the details of where he had been or who he had met. This bothered Paul at first, but then he realized: *It's for the best. This way I don't have to expose Rebecca, Hennley, Einstein, and the others to*

twelve

*ridicule by a bunch of cynics that don't even know what a wire stretcher is, much less how to use one.*

Ironically, it was Paul's parents who were most interested in the stories he had to share. Surprisingly, his hours with them were equally pleasant, if not more so than time spent with his friends. Indeed a new level of respect was born between Paul and Morris at breakfast one morning when Paul said, "I've been thinking, Dad, and I'd like to pay that woman's expenses for fixing her car."

Morris paused to sip his coffee and recover from his surprise before saying, "Her bills have already been paid."

"By you?"

"No, by Jason Medley's insurance company."

"Stitch's uncle?"

"Yes."

"How about the woman? Is she okay?"

"She's fine, Paul. It's good of you to ask, but you have no legal liability. You never did."

"I know. It's just that Mr. Vallenport has been paying me pretty well, and I wanted to clean up my debts . . . you know, clear my lie out of the air."

"That's an interesting way of putting it," Morris noted, pausing to sip from his cup again before adding, "and although it is true that you are not financially liable for Stitch's actions, you are morally responsible for your own."

"Just my point," said Paul.

Morris studied his son proudly and replied, "Then keep your money and pay your moral debts as you see fit. As your father, I can try to discipline you and hope you learn something along the way, but only you can reckon your moral accounts."

Paul grew thoughtful, then shook his head and grinned. "Spoken like a true lawyer, Dad."

"Thanks," Morris said wryly. "As for saving your money, Paul, you'll be driving soon and will need all the cash you can get your hands on."

Paul snorted.

"What?" wondered Morris.

"You just reminded me of one of the farmhands that refuses to drive. His name is Dundas Shoals. He's the original, original thinker."

The Shackleford family had just finished dinner and retired to the living room on the last night of Paul's visit home when he told his mother and father, "I'm proud of the strides in personal development you two have made in my absence. At this rate, you'll be normal soon."

"We're already normal," Morris countered, unable to suppress his amusement. "You're maturing, that's all."

"I do believe he is," observed Louise. "He seems

mighty antsy to get back and see that girl he's mentioned twice."

"Who?" Paul played dumb. "Inez?"

"No, the other one."

"Oh." Paul grinned slyly. "You must mean Vanessa."

"What your mother means, Paul, is you can't fool us," Morris said smugly. "You're glad we sent you to the Vallenports. Aren't you?"

"If that's what it took for you to grow up, then yes, Dad, I'm glad."

On Wednesday as Paul watched the world rolling by outside the bus window, he found himself thinking about Hennley Gray and all the pieces of information he had heard about the man. A vague and somewhat abstract impression of Hennley's personality was starting to form in Paul's mind . . . and he almost felt that he had known the man.

He was pondering this feeling when, out of

nowhere, it struck him that every time anyone on the farm had spoken about Hennley, they had done so privately, when no one else was around. Paul wondered about this for a while, and then, aware that he was only speculating, theorized that everyone was guarding their memories of Hennley. Maybe they had to because that was all they had left of the man who had made them feel important.

Hargrove was waiting in his car when Paul's bus pulled into Fenton that afternoon. As they drove Hargrove told Paul, "Ellis and Tucker cut and raked both hay fields on Monday. The hay should be dry enough to bale tomorrow. You ready for a long day?"

"Ready as I'm able," Paul replied gamely. Tucker had advised him that hay day always challenged one's endurance and Paul sort of knew what to expect.

"Louise and Morris doing well?"

"They're fine."

"And your city friends? They glad to see you?"

"Yes, sir," Paul replied, then laughed suddenly.

"Hmmm?" Hargrove wanted to know what was funny.

"I was just thinking how they all have their feet planted in midair."

"That's a good one." Hargrove smiled, and after driving a little ways in silence, cleared his throat and said, "So, Paul, Ada tells me you've taken an interest in Hennley Gray."

"I suppose I have. Yes, sir." Paul could not discern whether Hargrove approved or disapproved. The two of them had never discussed Hennley Gray.

As soon became apparent, Hargrove was eager to talk about his old friend. "That Hennley was a character. He knew exactly how to exasperate folks and get them thinking. It was a damn shame when we found him in the barn. He'd hidden himself pretty smartly . . .

was missing three days before Tucker's girl stumbled upon him."

"Rebecca?"

"Yeah. You know her?"

"We've met," Paul replied weakly. No one had told him that Rebecca found Hennley. It shocked Paul to think what a gruesome experience that must have been for her.

Hargrove evidently sensed that Paul needed a moment to think and did not speak for several minutes. Finally, he said, "I see you and Einstein have become friends. I'll tell you a story about him and Hennley, if you're interested."

"I am."

Hargrove cleared his throat again. "I'm fifty-six years old. In my time I've known many people that had dogs. Some had good relationships with their dogs, some of them had bad, but no one I ever met had a more striking relationship with their dog than the one Hennley had with Einstein. They were linked."

"How do you mean?"

Hargrove smiled. It was just the question he wanted. "They could transmit thoughts to each other."

Paul turned sideways and peered at Hargrove.

"I'm serious. Hennley could communicate with Einstein from a thousand yards away without ever raising his voice."

"Go on," Paul said.

Hargrove continued. "We used to raise chickens on the farm. They're all gone now, except for that one old rooster you see from time to time. Don't know why he's still alive. Anyhow, there was a coop on the knoll behind the hay barn. It had a good chicken wire fence around it, but we were losing a couple of hens every week. One day Hennley and I were back there when we saw a fat fox sitting right in the coop door. It was the oddest thing, but that fox looked at us and laughed."

Paul was more than a little incredulous. "It laughed?"

"It did." Hargrove nodded. "A cocky fox will do that. And as you might guess, it made us mad. I was ready to run for my gun, but then I heard Hennley whispering under his breath. He was saying, 'Einstein, you better come. We got a fox here that needs teaching a lesson.' I swear, that's what Hennley whispered, and no sooner did he finish whispering it than I heard Einstein give a yelp from across the road, nearly a quarter-mile away.

"That impressed me, so I just watched while Hennley made his way slowly to the gate in the fence. The fox was watching him too, but he didn't seem all that concerned, which was exactly what Hennley wanted. He just sidled toward the gate like he meant nothing, and about the time he got there I heard paws pattering up the blind side of the knoll. Then Hennley flung open the gate, Einstein shot by me at full speed and charged straight into the coop. That fox was so startled he couldn't collect himself to move before Einstein had him by the throat."

"Wow. He killed the fox?"

"No." The farm came into view as Hargrove answered. "The fox got away wounded, but he never came back for any more hens."

They stopped at the gate, and before Paul hopped from the car, Hargrove mused aloud, "Long as I live, I'll never forget Hennley whispering for Einstein to come teach that fox a lesson."

"That was a fascinating story, sir. I imagine there's plenty of good ones about Hennley and Einstein."

"They're a few," Hargrove allowed. "Shame you never got to meet Hennley. He had a way of making a lasting impression."

"Oh?" Paul said his tone, practically begging the man to elaborate.

Yet Hargrove had abruptly withdrawn into a world of private memories and only muttered, "He's a hard one to forget."

The crew started in the large field at eight o'clock sharp. Tucker drove the big Allis-Chalmers tractor to which the baler was attatched. A fabulous product of American ingenuity, the baler gathered up the raked hay, compressed it into rectangular bundles, tied the bundles tightly with twine, and spit them neatly onto the ground. The bales were then lifted by hand and thrown onto a wagon that was periodically moved around the field for easier access.

Almost any teenage person can lift and hoist a single bale of hay from the ground onto the back of a wagon while standing in a hot, shadeless field, but

thirteen

with baling hay, it's not the one bale that undoes the person, it's the thirtieth, or the fortieth, or maybe the fifty-second.

Paul, having worked on the farm for three weeks in June while dining on Inez Button's all-you-can-eat-and-more diet, had developed more muscle tone and increased his stamina. That was good, for otherwise he could never have kept pace with the men. Even at that, it took all his willpower not to fall behind, or indeed, fall over in a faint.

Fortunately for Paul, the wagon was stacked to full capacity by ten-thirty and the crew took a water break before hauling the hay to the barn. The temperature was in the upper eighties and itchy hay dust clung to everyone like glue. Paul filled a paper cup and sat on the tailgate of the green farm truck beside Ellis. They'd been sitting ten seconds when Einstein emerged from under the vehicle, looked Ellis in the eye, lifted a leg, and peed on the left rear tire. Ellis huffed derisively.

"He just does that to irritate me. He wouldn't do it if I didn't mind."

Paul looked at Einstein and could not refrain from laughing. The dog was actually smirking at Ellis.

Paul drank from his cup, then said to Ellis, "I've been wondering. Einstein follows the truck because he thinks that's where Hennley will go if he comes back to the farm. Why doesn't he wait at the cottage? They lived there together, right?"

Ellis nodded and answered, "Despite his many personality defects, that dog has a mind like a steel trap. He remembers the last time he saw Hennley, and that was getting out of the truck in the barn lot. He did go back and check the cottage once or twice right after Hennley died, but since then, he's put all his eggs in the truck."

Paul mused a moment, then said, "Your dad told me a pretty amazing story about Hennley and Einstein."

"The one about the fox in the chicken coop?"

"Yeah."

Ellis quaffed his water and stared thoughtfully across the field. "Dad and Hennley were the same age, you know."

Paul shook his head. That was news to him.

"I was five when Hennley came here. In a way, Hennley was like a second father to me."

"How?"

"Well . . . I always looked up to him."

"Oh, what kind of person was he?"

Ellis replied without hesitation, "Firm with the reins. Nothing flustered him. He'd get weary sometimes, but he never lost control."

"Weary about what?"

"I don't know. Life. People disappointed him. He always felt everybody could do better than they did. He wasn't a grump about it, but you knew when Hennley was unhappy."

"Was that often?"

"No more than most people." Ellis wiped hay dust from his nose, then said, "I've never known what to think about Dad's fox story . . . although there was definitely something unusual between Einstein and Hennley."

Paul looked at Einstein, who still stood by the left tire, apparently listening to everything that was said. "You mean, they were mentally linked?"

Ellis glanced over to where Dundas and Tucker were sitting in a pool of shade by the wagon and slipped off the tailgate of the truck. "I don't know. Just too many coincidences that logic won't explain. Anyhow . . . let's haul that wagon to the barn and see if we can get it loaded again before lunch."

It was ninety-three humid degrees when the crew started in the smaller field shortly after two o'clock. Two hours later, they had about half the hay up when Paul (who could hardly believe he was still standing) saw Ellis's truck drive up and park by the entrance to the field. The driver-side door opened and Maya appeared with a wicker basket. The passenger-side door opened and Rebecca Dyson stepped out with a five-gallon thermos in her hands.

Tucker shut off the tractor when he saw the pair, and as if on cue, everyone ceased working and headed toward a shady spot on the south side of the field. Greetings were exchanged all around and Maya pulled a blanket from her basket, which she spread on the ground before setting out cups, muffins, and cookies, and telling the group, "Inez thought you might need a pick-me-up."

"A week off would be more like it," Tucker joked.

"Or a cold bath," adjoined Ellis.

Everyone settled on the blanket, except Dundas. He served himself a cup of ice tea and went to stand alone in a second patch of shade a dozen or so yards away. As the group nibbled on muffins and cookies,

Paul threw discreet glances at Rebecca. She was sitting by her father, with whom she clearly felt very comfortable . . . and toward whom Paul now felt a small (and, he knew, absurd) pang of envy. He and Rebecca eventually made direct eye contact, yet just as they did, something beyond Paul caught her attention and her face filled with alarm. He turned to where she was looking and saw Dundas sinking to his knees. The man had dropped his cup and put his hands on his ears, and after his knees hit the ground, he fell over in a faint.

Ellis and Tucker also saw Dundas fall and rushed to his side. When Paul and Rebecca arrived behind the men, Dundas's eyes were rolled back in his head and he was moaning. Ellis got behind Dundas, grabbed him under the arms, and lifted him into a sitting position. Tucker squatted and gently patted the man's cheek. "Ho, now, Dundas. What's the problem?"

Dundas continued to moan as if wounded.

"Paul, fetch the water jug from the truck."

As Paul hurried to do Ellis's bidding, he saw that Einstein had crawled out from under the truck and was trotting into the woods on the west side of the hay field. Paul didn't pause to wonder where Einstein was going. He grabbed the water jug and ran back to the group.

Tucker took the jug from Paul, unscrewed the cap, and poured a portion of its contents over Dundas's head. In the meantime, Maya had come forward with a cup. Tucker filled it with water and held it to Dundas's lips. The man ceased moaning, grabbed the proffered cup, wriggled for Ellis to release him, and drank.

"You all right now, Dundas?"

"What happened?"

Dundas blinked, then surveyed the surrounding group with a slow sweep of his head and said, "It was Hennley. He spoke to me. Then I guess I passed out."

"You saw him?" Rebecca asked in a trembling voice.

Dundas shook his head. "No. I just heard his voice."

"What did he say?" Tucker took the words out of Paul's and everyone else's mind and mouth.

Paul stiffened when Dundas looked directly at him and paused before answering. It seemed to Paul the man was preparing to address him personally. Just before he spoke, Dundas lowered his gaze and quoted, "'Fight your demons while they're little folks. If you don't, they'll grow up to be monsters. Then you'll never lick them.' That's what Hennley said."

Ellis furrowed his brow and looked into the air around him as if trying to detect Hennley's presence.

"Was that all he said?" Maya asked calmly.

Dundas nodded gravely.

Tucker sighed ponderously, then shrugged. "Sounds like something Hennley would say."

"It was him," Dundas assured Tucker. "His voice was just as gravelly as it always was."

"Durn," Tucker said softly. "If he was here, I wish he'd said hello to me."

Paul took a deep breath, then looked at Rebecca. Her arms were crossed in front of her and she was peering intensely at Dundas with her blue-blue eyes. She did not appear to be doubting the man, but rather, trying to see if there was anything else hidden in his heart.

Paul didn't know what to think. He was still reeling from the eerie notion that Dundas, and thereby Hennley, had spoken to him. *Was my little lie a demon?* Paul's deepest inner self wondered. *Am I supposed to fight that before it grows into a monster? Was the voice that spoke to Dundas the one I heard in the storm? Was it Hennley who whispered to me?*

The last of the hay was in the barn by a quarter to six that evening. By seven o'clock Paul had showered and ravenously downed dinner. Afterward he hobbled onto the veranda and sank into a cushioned chair. His joints ached, and every muscle in his body was bruised with fatigue. When he saw Granny shuffling out to join him, he told her, "I think I know how if feels to be old, Granny."

"Do you?" She smirked and settled in the chair beside Paul. "One day of haying is nothing. Try having three children and watching two of them turn fifty."

fourteen

"Sorry," Paul said repentantly. "I didn't mean to compare."

Granny's smirk softened. "No doubt you're tired."

Tired and vicariously aged though Paul may have felt, he was anticipating the next few days with enthusiasm. Specifically, he looked forward to the day after tomorrow, when he and Rebecca Dyson had a ten o'clock appointment to meet by the elm trees at the head of the ridge road. They had spoken briefly in the hay field after Dundas had fainted, and she had asked if he would accompany her to the cottage. Of course, he had told her yes, and although at the time he did not ask why, he had sensed her desire to go there had been precipitated by Dundas's assertion that Hennley was near.

A somewhat bland, undistinguished sunset unfolded as Granny and Paul sat facing the mountains. "You haven't seen Einstein, have you?" Granny inquired after a while.

"Not since this afternoon. He was in the hay field with us, but he took off. Are you worried about him?"

"Only curious. Ada mentioned he wasn't waiting when she put out his supper bowl. It's not like Einstein to miss a meal."

As Paul recalled seeing Einstein trotting away from the truck when he'd gone to fetch the water jug, it suddenly occurred to him that the dog had departed while Dundas was still semiconscious. *Had Einstein sensed Hennley's passing presence and followed after him?*

"Are you all right?" Granny asked Paul. "You look upset."

"I, ah . . . had a strange thought. I'm fine now. But may I ask you, was Hennley ever married?"

"That was your thought?"

"No. It's just something I've been wondering."

"Hennley was married briefly before he moved to the farm. Very briefly. In fact, his marriage only lasted three weeks before it was annulled."

"Three weeks," Paul remarked with surprise. "And the whole time he lived here, he lived alone?"

"Until he got Einstein," Granny replied, then volunteered, "Hennley had a few women friends from time to time, and I suspect at least one of them would've gone to the altar with him. But knowing Hennley — and extending the meaning of something he said once — I believe he was reluctant to make vows again that he might not be able to keep. It's only my theory, but I think he was ashamed of publicly committing to a promise that was void in three weeks. He didn't want to risk breaking his word again."

Paul didn't think that was right. "He shouldn't have felt ashamed if what went wrong wasn't his fault."

Granny chuckled. "The world wouldn't be the world we live in if people could think for others. Hennley knew who he was and why. He did what he saw fit."

"He cared that much about his word?"

"I believe he did."

Paul contemplated the extreme nature of Hennley's character and wondered if he could live up to the man's lofty self-standard.

The evening sky began to darken and Granny got up from her chair. Paul jumped to his feet and preceded her to the door. "Here, I'll get it for you."

"No need. I've been going through that door since before you were born."

"Please, allow me. I'm headed upstairs anyway. I'm beat."

Paul's body rejoiced in the restorative repose of sleep the second he hit the bed. His mind, however, still had a tiny amount of energy to burn. It did so, replaying moments from the remarkable day that was now ending: *Fight your demons while they're little folks. If you don't, they'll grow up to be monsters. Then you'll never lick them.*

*He was firm with the reins. Nothing flustered him.*

*See you at the elm trees on Saturday. Ten o'clock.*

Then a distant crowing of the fugitive rooster somewhere in the valley below interrupted his memories.

Finally, before dreamland, he had a last run-on thought: *Hennley Gray worked here twenty-five years he was not famous anywhere else I wonder where Einstein went.*

Everyone expressed more curiosity than open concern when Friday morning arrived without any sign of Einstein. Paul thought, or rather hoped, that Ellis was correct when he said, "It's been more than a year now. Maybe Einstein figured out that Hennley isn't coming back and went gallivanting. He used to do that now and then when Hennley was alive."

Paul told everyone at the post-breakfast meeting that he'd seen Einstein leaving the hay field the day before, yet did not voice the bizarre notion he'd had about Einstein pursuing Hennley's spirit trail. He wasn't

## fifteen

afraid of being ridiculed. He just didn't think it would do any good, even if he was right.

Paul spent the day helping Ellis and Tucker move feed corn from the silo to the barn, shoveling the corn into the grinder and bagging the milled grain. That was outwardly. Inwardly he vacillated between fretting about Einstein and anticipating his upcoming rendezvous with Rebecca. The disparity of the feelings generated by these two mental activities was immense, and by the end of the day Paul was not only physically spent, but emotionally strained as well.

He went for a short stroll that evening after supper, and when he was well away from the house and sure that no one could see him, he tried to achieve with Einstein what Hennley had done in Hargrove's story about the fox in the chicken coop. Although Paul did not expect results, he put his heart into the effort.

"Wherever you are, Einstein, better come home

now. There's a bunch of people here who miss you. I know I do," he whispered.

Paul stood silently for ten minutes or more, listening for a howled response that never came.

"Just come on home where you're loved. I'll sneak you a ham steak if you do."

On Saturday, Rebecca was there ahead of him, leaning against one of the elm trees. She'd kicked off her shoes and was standing barefoot on a patch of moss. She wore jeans and a long-sleeved T-shirt pushed up to her elbows. "Thanks for coming," she said as Paul approached.

"Me?" Paul pointed at his chest with a thumb. "It's my pleasure."

Rebecca slipped on her shoes, and they started along the ridge road. During the first hundred or so yards of their journey together, Paul tried a couple of times to launch a casual conversation, and although Rebecca replied in some manner to each of his comments, he soon recognized that she was in a thinking mood, not a talking one. Respectfully, he desisted with his small talk and withdrew into the company of his own thoughts. His tact evidently met with Rebecca's approval, for she soon flashed an appreciative, blue-eyed smile in his direction.

After they passed through the gate, walked down through the swale, and entered the cottage yard, Rebecca went to sit on the bench. Paul stood nearby, watching her contemplate the little house. He still did not know why they were there, but knew he would find out soon and was content admiring Rebecca's profile while he waited.

She was unlike any other person he'd ever known. Some of what made her different, he knew, was her farm-girl upbringing. Yet Paul was also beginning to understand that people were people, no matter where they lived . . . be it the desert or the jungle, in the city or on a farm.

Rebecca soon turned to Paul and announced, "I haven't been inside since the last time Dad and I visited Hennley. That was Easter, more than a year and three months ago."

Paul put on his best listening face. Rebecca was obviously preparing to tell him something.

After a thoughtful pause, she said, "I want to go in today. I'm hoping you'll go with me."

"Of course."

Rebecca stood, reached into a hip pocket, and withdrew a key. Apprehension was written large on her face, and when she hesitated in place, Paul touched her elbow and cocked his head toward the cottage. She took his cue and they walked side by side to the door. Rebecca handed the key to Paul. "I'll go in first if you open it. I hope the lock hasn't rusted."

"I'm sure it's fine," Paul said in a reassuring tone. He was hoping to calm Rebecca as well as himself. He inserted the key into the slot and rotated it clockwise. The lock clicked opened.

They were greeted by a wall of musty air as they entered. Paul propped the door open with a rock that had been left on the stoop for that purpose. Rebecca went to the front windows, drew aside the sun-bleached curtains, and lifted both sashes. There was a third window in the far wall, and after Paul opened it, fresh air began ventilating through the cottage.

The front room was set up as a combination kitchen, dining room, and living area. Each of three interior doors was partially open. One led to a bedroom, the other into a bathroom, and the third onto a glassed-in porch. Handwoven rugs covered most of the floor in the front room, where there was a wood-stove for heat, a gas stove for cooking, a refrigerator, and a round oak table with two straight-back chairs. An aged, white envelope lay upon the table.

As Rebecca quietly surveyed the main room, Paul sensed she needed to be alone with her feelings and wandered onto the enclosed porch. He saw a broom, a vacuum cleaner, a shelf stacked with dusty books, an easy chair, a lamp, and a tattered couch. Paul inspected the books, all of which he soon realized were either biographies or histories. Evidently, Hennley had been interested in the past.

Paul turned and was about to withdraw from the porch when a framed photograph hanging on the wall behind the easy chair caught his eye. Unable to resist, Paul crossed to the black-and-white print and saw a scruffy-looking, slightly taller than average, middle-aged man. He wore boots, work pants, and a buttoned shirt with the sleeves rolled up to the elbows. He was standing in a plowed field beside a puppy-faced Einstein. Paul knew instinctively that he was looking at a picture of Hennley Gray.

There was something relaxed and unpolished

about the man, and although Paul did not see a striking resemblance between himself and Hennley, he
could understand how someone might perceive a sim-
ilarity. To Paul, the most notable quality about the man
in the picture was the patient, slightly put-upon look
in his eyes as he stared into the camera. Hennley Gray
appeared to be thinking, *I'll stand for one picture, but
that's all you get.*

When Paul returned to the main room, Rebecca
was sitting at the oak table, clutching the envelope
with both hands. Her expression said one thing and
one thing only: *I am sad.*

Paul moved slowly across the room and sat in the
empty chair beside Rebecca. She ended the silence
with a rush of words. "Dad and everyone else checked
here when Hennley disappeared, but the place was
locked and his truck was parked by the barn, and no
one thought there was a need to break in the place. I
don't know if Mr. Vallenport came here before he

got Hennley's package in the mail. Maybe he did." Rebecca paused to study the letters of her name printed on the envelope. She drew a deep breath and exhaled loudly. "I suppose it doesn't really matter when this was left for me. I have it now."

Paul waited ten seconds. "It's a letter?"

"I think so."

"Are you going to read it?"

"I have to . . . don't I?"

"That's up to you."

Rebecca bit her bottom lip, blinked, then stood and told Paul, "Let's close the windows and lock up. I'll read it outside."

Paul followed Rebecca to the bench and sat a respectful distance away. Curious hardly described what Paul
was feeling. A ten-page poem would be needed to ap-
proximate what was going on in Rebecca's heart and
mind.

She opened the envelope, removed two folded
sheets of paper, and said softly to Paul. "You can read
it with me if you want."

Paul started with surprise. "You don't mind?"

"No, not if you want to read it."

Paul slid closer to Rebecca and together they
read the hand-printed letter that Hennley Gray had

sixteen

composed more than a year ago. The handwriting was bold, without flourishes, and easy to read.

Dear Rebecca,

I will be gone by the time you read this. Please do not weep for me. I acted with a clear conscience. I know Ada told you I was ill inside with cancer and asked you to keep that news private. Thank you for doing so.

I loved life, Rebecca. Dying brings me no joy, and yet for me it is not so terrifying as you might think. My choice was simple: Wait for the sickness to take me slowly, or move to the finish line on my own terms. You know how I was about guarding my own terms in life. It only follows that I should guard them to my end.

Hargrove has probably told you by now that I left the cottage to you. This is why I did what I did away from my home, so it will not be marred with the memory of a death. It is not much in the way of property. Sell it if you wish. I hope you will keep it for when you are older and desire a tranquil retreat from the world. You are young now, and tranquility may seem of little value, but I predict it will mean more to you later in life.

I have left a small sum of money for you and Catherine. It will come to each of you when you reach eighteen. Like the cottage, do with it as you wish.

Before I go, allow me to beg a favor and give you some advice. They are both the same: Always listen to the wisdom in your heart. Your heart will guide you through times of confusion and protect you from distracting fools. People who know their hearts know themselves. They are the lucky ones.

Again, I bid you not to weep for me. I will look over you and everyone on the farm if I can.

                                    Love ever after,
                                    Hennley


Paul sat back and watched Rebecca reread what was written. He could only marvel at the concentration pouring from her eyes as they passed over the printed words.

*The letter is clear and to the point,* Paul thought. Just as he had come to imagine Hennley Gray.

After Rebecca again came to Hennley's salutation she neatly folded the pages, returned them to the envelope, and heaved a sorrowful, stress-relieving sigh. "Hennley said not to weep for him, so I won't. Not anymore."

For a second or two Paul feared he might cry, but he soon struggled past that emotion and told Rebecca, "I think you are very brave."

Rebecca eyed the cottage and said nothing.

"Hennley must have been brave too," Paul continued. "It had to test his courage, writing such a calm letter on the eve of his . . . last day."

Rebecca withdrew her gaze from the cottage and peered at Paul. "I'm sorry for involving you in all this. The whole situation must seem too weird to you."

"No, it's been very interesting for me, getting to know Hennley, and I feel that I have. In fact, I've probably been a bit nosy about the man, asking everyone questions and all. He must have been great. Everyone here remembers him so fondly."

"Yes, he was great," Rebecca said softly. "And I'll be the first to admit, Paul, I can't seem to get him off my mind."

As Paul nodded in understanding to Rebecca, he recalled that she and Maya had been discussing memory and the subconscious mind when he found them in Ellis's yard before his trip home. During the silent spell that now ensued, he pondered the manner in which memories were made and then nurtured in the mind . . . and how the stronger ones served to connect the past with the present . . . like the history books on Hennley's shelf and Einstein's daily pursuit of the old, green truck.

Paul turned after a while and asked Rebecca, "The other day in the hay field when Dundas said Hennley had spoken to him, what did you think?"

Rebecca shrugged. "I thought it could be true."

"You believe there's a ghost?"

Rebecca shrugged again. "I'm not convinced there isn't one, nor do I know for certain there is. I guess I agree with my dad on that question. I've been thinking about Hennley every day for the past year, but so far I haven't seen any ghosts."

Paul pursed his lips and looked thoughtful.

"Of course all that may change next Saturday."

The look on Paul's face became a *what*?

"Oh, right. I was planning to tell you. Maya wants

to hold a séance next week at Ellis's house. She asked me to invite you. Seven o'clock on Saturday."

The *what* on Paul's face became an incredulous *do what*? "A séance?"

Despite having just read Hennley's letter, Rebecca was amused enough by the look on Paul's face to laugh. "You know what a séance is, don't you?"

"Yeah. I, ah . . . you talk to the dead."

"You try," said Rebecca, adding, "Maya is very spiritual. She doesn't claim to be a clairvoyant or anything, but she's held séances before and says it will work if Hennley's soul is still on the farm."

"You mean, his ghost?"

Rebecca nodded. "And if he is here, we want to know why . . . and tell him that he's free to go."

Paul retreated into silence and considered what he had just been told. If Rebecca had not been sitting there looking him in the eye, he would have doubted her seriousness. As it was, his mind was open.

Rebecca stood, put the cottage key in the envelope with Hennley's letter, and slipped them in a hip pocket. She smiled wanly at Paul and gestured toward the ridge road. "Shall we?"

They were in the honeysuckle swale when Rebecca said, "Thank you again for going in the cottage with me. I didn't want to go alone, but I didn't want to take someone that knew Hennley and might get upset."

"That makes sense," Paul replied simply. Although entering Hennley's vacated abode had not upset him, it had stirred up emotions that Paul did not fully comprehend.

When they reached the gate, Rebecca told Paul, "The séance is kind of a secret. Not everyone on the farm is invited, so if you don't mind, if anyone asks why you're going to Ellis's next Saturday, just say we're having dinner."

Paul grew suddenly troubled. "I, ah . . . that creates a dilemma for me, Rebecca. I never told you what happened before I came here. The details don't really matter now, but lately I've been on a campaign to tell the truth. Not that I never told the truth before, but, well, it's kind of a long story. . . . and I —"

"It's okay. You don't have to explain." Rebecca cut Paul off in mid-sentence. "It was wrong of me to ask you to lie."

Paul hesitated a second, then asked, "Are we going to have dinner first?"

"Yes. That's the plan."

Paul opened the gate, held it for Rebecca, and allowed with a hint of philosophical amusement, "Well, then, if that's the case, it wouldn't technically be a lie to say so."

By Monday when Einstein had not reappeared at the house, the growing concern over his whereabouts became grave. By Tuesday, that gravity had taken on a depressing weight and everyone was fearing the worst. Hargrove took the matter seriously enough to stay home on Tuesday and ride around the farm and surrounding area with Ellis in the green truck. They rode all day, exploring every sector of land where the vehicle could pass, honking and hollering for Einstein to come. In the course of their search they discovered two stray calves that no one had known were missing,

seventeen

but as Hargrove said sadly when he and Ellis returned to the house that evening, "We saw neither hide nor hair of the old fellow."

Paul spent the week in a sort of black-and-blue funk. Einstein had become his closest confidant and friend on the farm, and Paul suffered the same helpless anguish over his absence as everyone who had known and associated him in their hearts with Hennley.

On Friday night, Paul awoke suddenly in the wee hours of darkness. Either he'd been dreaming or he had heard Einstein howling in the distance. Paul rolled out of bed, stumbled to his bedroom window, lifted the screen, and stuck his head outside. A light breeze rustled over the fields and through the one tree in the yard. Otherwise, the world was quiet.

Paul continued to listen and soon — so faintly he did not know if he should trust his own ears — he heard a canine voice rising above the mountains.

*Aaouuuuu,* the voice called out, then fell silent. Paul waited to hear the cry again. Nothing came, and after a few minutes he returned to bed.

It was now Saturday evening and Paul had just stepped out of a hot shower. There was a full-length mirror in the bathroom, and as Paul towel-dried himself, he idly admired the reflection of his naked body. He knew he was unlikely to be mistaken for a man as Inez Buttons intended, but still, he had put on a pound or two of muscle and was no longer the beanpole she had first encountered.

When Paul exited the house he saw Granny and Ada sitting on the veranda. "Have fun," offered Granny, and Ada added, "I'll leave the back door unlocked."

"I will," Paul told Granny. "Thanks," he said to Ada. He knew they knew where he was going, and probably why — secrets did not live long on the

162

Vallenports' farm — and was appreciatively aware of their discretion on the subject.

Rebecca and Paul entered Ellis's front yard at the same moment. He'd never seen her wearing a skirt before, or with her hair gathered at the back of her neck, and he was struck anew by her beauty. In a flash he forgot all his anxieties about the séance. "Hello, Rebecca."

"Hi, Paul."

"So here we are."

"It appears that way." Rebecca smiled brightly.

Together they climbed the porch steps and knocked on the front door of Ellis's house.

"Great. You're right on time. Come, come," Maya welcomed them warmly, whirling in the hallway and gesturing for them to follow her toward the kitchen.

Ellis was at the counter, grating Parmesan cheese onto a plate as Maya swept the guests into the room. Salutations were exchanged, and then Ellis tugged at the apron he wore over a tie-dyed T-shirt and warned

Paul with feigned gruffness, "If anyone teases me about this at work, I'll know how they found out."

"I won't say a word."

Maya giggled and put an arm around Ellis's waist. "I think an apron becomes him. Don't you, Rebecca?"

"Very domestic," Rebecca noted.

"See, Ellis," Maya chimed, "she agrees."

During the course of dinner (a pasta-and-pesto concoction that Inez Buttons would never have permitted in her kitchen) Paul was won over by Maya's fluid, conversational style. She was quick-witted and kind and saw to it that he felt included and comfortable at the table. It was also interesting for Paul to see Ellis in his home, with his high school sweetheart at his side. Paul had already noted that Ellis was a man of shifting moods, and the one on display this evening was gregarious, lighthearted, and surprisingly tender.

After dinner, Paul helped Rebecca remove the dishes from the table and carry them to the kitchen sink. He did so with mounting wariness about what was coming next. No one, as far as he could recollect, had mentioned or even alluded to the ultimate purpose of their gathering. Doubting that the plans had changed, Paul presumed they shared his rising apprehension about attempting to communicate with a man whose ashes had been scattered to the wind.

*What if we do reach Hennley?* Paul wondered. *Will I recognize his voice from the storm? Does Hennley know where Einstein has gone?*

Four straight-back chairs were set around a card table in the living room. A wooden cutting block was on the table. On the block stood a squat candle. As Ellis lit the candle and turned off the overhead light, Maya lit a stick of sandalwood incense and placed it in a ceramic holder on the mantelpiece. Afterward she sat, then gestured for Rebecca to sit across from her, Ellis to sit on her left, and Paul on her right.

With everyone settled, Maya said in a reverent

tone, "We are here tonight hoping to communicate with Hennley Gray's soul. In seeking to contact him, we must clear our minds, release our egos, and become conduits between this world and the next."

Paul thought that was a pretty serious opening and peeked at Rebecca for signs of what she might be thinking. Her face was a neutral mask. She was listening without judging. Paul redirected his attention to Maya, who was saying, "The realm of spirit entities exists everywhere around us. It is only the density of our emotional bodies and the clutter in our minds that separates us from that realm. Empty your minds of that clutter. Let it fall away until nothing remains."

Maya spread her fingers and placed her hands thumb to thumb on the cutting block. Everyone followed suit. Then she resumed speaking in a low-pitched, hypnotic voice, "Let us close our eyes so that our lashes touch and we can still see the candle's flame. Let the flame consume our doubts and fears . . .

and listen for the quiet speech of the hidden. Breathe in harmony and think of Hennley. We think welcoming thoughts. . . . We think he is here among us. . . . We are mediums through which his soul may speak."

After Maya ceased speaking, the only sound in the room was of four people breathing. Paul could not resist examining the faces around the table. Ellis's closed eyes were hooded in shadow and his dark head shimmered in the candlelight. Maya squinted intently at the burning flame. Rebecca's face was serenely composed.

Maya whispered, "We listen for you, Hennley. We are conduits for your words. Speak if you are here."

*I'm a conduit,* thought Paul, returning his attention to the flame and breathing in concert with the group. He was trying to void his mind of thought when he recalled Hennley writing in his letter to Rebecca that he would watch over her and everyone on the farm if he could. Paul suddenly became aware of a minute, bioelectrical charge entering him through Rebecca's fingertip.

Paul willed himself to listen and believe. He breathed with the group. He gradually began to drift out of himself.

Seconds passed. . . . Then slowly but surely Paul's consciousness was absorbed by something larger than himself. It was an inexplicable something, an almost tactile silence that rippled through the air and wove everyone at the table into one.

"Hennley," Maya whispered. Or thought.

The silence grew palpable and the hairs on the back of Paul's neck stood up and tingled. He felt or imagined a fifth presence enter in the room. He heard a low *grrring* sound.

*What was that?*

Paul and everyone else at the table nearly jumped out of their skin when an echoing yowl reverberated in their ears. After Paul landed back in his seat and his heart started thumping again, he whirled around and saw a dark shape pressing against the window screen.

For a moment, time stopped. Then Paul jumped from his seat and hurried from the living room. Ellis was right behind him, and as they were passing through the hallway toward the front door, Paul could hear Rebecca laughing. It was a musical sound that resonated perfectly with how Paul was feeling.

"Einstein!" Paul fell to his knees and threw his arms around the prodigal creature.

"Where've you been, you devil?" Ellis knelt beside Paul and rubbed under Einstein's chin.

Einstein said nothing. He just sat there tolerating the outpouring of love with grim forbearance.

Then Ellis guffawed and Paul began to laugh. They were both so relieved the dog was home, they gladly forgave him the anguish his absence had caused.

Rebecca and Maya came out to welcome Einstein home, and then, after he ate the large bowl of scraps that Ellis brought and absorbed all the affection he was in the mood to receive, he excused himself from the porch and trotted off into the night. Presumably he was headed up to the big house to check in with the green farm truck.

A short while later, Rebecca and Paul thanked Maya and Ellis for dinner and the interesting evening, and said good night. They were descending the porch steps together when Rebecca said to Paul, "Walk me home?"

"I was hoping you'd ask."

They left the parking lot and turned right on the

eighteen

paved road leading past the hay barn. "So, what'd you think of the séance?" Paul wondered. "Until the end, I mean."

"I thought we might be getting somewhere."

"Me too. It felt like something was happening just before Einstein interrupted us."

"Want to know what I really thought?" asked Rebecca.

"Of course I do."

"Two things," Rebecca began. "One, I kept telling myself that anything is possible, and that if Hennley spoke to us I would believe it. But then, second, I was thinking it wasn't fair of us to be calling him. I mean, if his soul is out there, we shouldn't tug at it the way we were doing. Does that make sense?"

"Sort of," Paul allowed. "Do you mean it's not Hennley haunting the farm, but everyone else haunting him?"

"I hadn't thought of it that way, but yes."

"Want to know something I thought?"

"Certainly."

"Well, the way Einstein snuck up to the window and barked right at the most suspenseful moment, it reminded me of something Mr. Vallenport told me. Have you heard him tell the story about Hennley and Einstein and the fox in the chicken coop?"

"I've heard the story from Dad."

"Oh, then you know the point about Einstein and Hennley being so linked they could read each other's minds."

"Mr. Vallenport said that?"

"Maybe not in those exact words, but yes, that's what he told me."

"Hmmm."

"So anyway, my thought was, right after Einstein barked, I wondered if they were still connected and Einstein had been drawn to the porch by Hennley's presence."

Rebecca walked a ways before replying, "I must say, Paul, I like the way your mind works."

Fortunately it was night, and though a first quarter-moon shed a pale light upon the pair, Rebecca could not see Paul's face. Her words had hit him where it counts and he was blushing.

They turned right again onto the dirt road that skirted the cornfield and led eventually to Rebecca's house. "Paul?"

"Yes."

"Does everything on the farm seem crazy to you?"

"Not really."

"Honestly? The way we hang on to our memories and go chasing after dead folks, we don't seem crazy?"

"No, honestly, you don't. In fact, to me it seems that everyone here is exactly who they are and they don't pretend to be who they aren't. That makes you different from most of my friends back home, but it doesn't make any of you crazy." Paul paused for a second or two before adding, "With the possible exception of Dundas Shoals."

"Good ol' Dundas. He tries to hide it, but he really cares deeply about everyone. It wouldn't surprise me if he made up the whole story about the ghost just to give us all hope of seeing Hennley again."

"That's an interesting theory," Paul declared. "I like the way your mind works too, Rebecca."

"Thank you," Rebecca said sincerely. "Here's another theory for you. Part of what I believe keeps everyone on the farm living in the past is a lack of options. I mean, there isn't much change around here. You're the first new thing to happen for a while."

"Thing?"

Rebecca laughed. "Sorry, I meant person. And friend. To be honest, Paul, I don't always click with people my age. It's been nice meeting someone I can talk with."

"That goes ditto for me," Paul gushed, expressing but a fragment of what he was feeling inside.

They rounded a bend in the road and Rebecca's home came into view. It was a two-story, wood-frame structure similar to Ellis's house, only smaller and more modest in scope. Rebecca stopped and informed Paul, "I'm fine from here. It was kind of you to walk me this far."

"It was my pleasure."

"I'll see you," she said, yet instead of departing she hesitated in place and looked at Paul.

"I hope soon," he replied, and then before he quite knew what he was saying, added, "Good-bye for now."

"Bye," she said, turning and walking away.

Paul winced as he watched her go, regretting that he had not leaned over and kissed her when she lingered. "I'm sure she wanted me to kiss her," he muttered under his breath. "I'm pretty sure."

He was still standing where Rebecca had left him when she turned and called, "Maybe next Saturday, if you're free, we'll go up to the cottage. I want to sort through Hennley's books."

"I'll be free," Paul shouted. "And if I'm not, I'll go anyway."

"Ten o'clock then? By the elm trees."

"Ten o'clock."

Paul's thoughts danced in his head as he returned along the dirt road. He was about halfway between the bend and the paved road when he was startled by a rustling sound in the woods to his left. He turned and gazed tensely toward the sound . . . and soon saw a shadow racing in his direction. Although it wasn't large, it was coming fast, and coming straight at him.

Paul was about to leap sideways when the scrawny old farm rooster broke across the road in front of him and darted into the field to his right. It neither crowed nor squawked nor even looked at Paul. The rogue bird just shot into the night and disappeared.

A minute passed before Paul recovered his composure and laughed. He was tickled because Rebecca was his friend, because Einstein had come home, and because he was put in mind of the proverbial riddle: *Why did the chicken cross the road?*

Although Paul didn't really care what motivated the chicken, he contemplated the riddle all the way through the valley, past the fork, and up the long hill to the house. An answer came to him as he reached the parking lot and he said aloud, "I bet a fox was after that rooster."

Einstein poked his head out from under the truck when he heard Paul speak, and Paul went over to give him a good-night scratch.

In the days and weeks after Einstein's return, there was much speculation about where he had gone and what he had done while he was away. The theories, for the most part, were presented in a jocular vein, and each one of them was punctuated with relief that the dog was home.

During the same period, it seemed to Paul, everyone on the farm was more lighthearted and quick to laugh than they had been all summer. That is, everyone except Dundas, who appeared to become more obtuse and distant. For instance, when he overheard talk about the aborted séance at Ellis's house he

nineteen

scoffed and told Ellis, "Only fools make games out of the next world. You should know better."

While Dundas was embittered by rumors of the séance, Inez Buttons was fascinated, and she pressed Paul relentlessly for details of the evening. After he eventually yielded and told her what he had experienced, she then pestered him daily to repeat the part about the hair standing up on the back of his neck. Paul knew she was teasing him, yet she seemed to derive so much joy from his tale that he humbly obliged her requests.

There was a third matter that Paul never heard discussed yet imagined was the source of some speculation on the farm: his relationship with Rebecca Dyson. Week by week, they were spending more and more time together, and since nearly all that time was spent openly in fields, or sitting on fences or porches, or walking along well-traveled roads, their growing intimacy was not the least bit secret. Even so, Paul never overheard any gossip about him and Rebecca, nor was he asked any questions. At times, he half wished Tucker would bring up the subject so he could reply (honestly) that nothing inappropriate had ever occurred between his daughter and himself. But Tucker never mentioned the matter. Paul was not really disappointed by the man's silence. After all, a half-wish goes both ways.

And so the final days of summer marched by . . . and almost before Paul knew what had happened, he awoke one morning with the knowledge that this was his last Friday on the Vallenports' farm. He was not alone in this knowledge, and at breakfast that day Inez remarked, "I did my best. You aren't quite a man yet, but I reckon you're big enough to discourage the bullies when you go back to school."

Paul was surprised by his own emotion. "I'll miss you, Inez."

"And me, you." Inez looked away quickly.

They were saved from any further gush by

Dundas, who poked his head into the kitchen and told Paul, "If you're coming with us, come on."

Paul crammed a square of cornbread into his mouth before hurrying out through the garage. He knew Dundas was deeply distressed about the fever Vanessa had been running for the past few days and did not want to keep him waiting. Tucker was outside in the green truck. He had just returned to the farm with the antibiotics Dundas ordered from the vet.

They beat Einstein through the gate, and after Dundas jumped back into the rear of the truck he banged anxiously on the cab roof. "Step on it, Tucker. Let's go."

"He loves that pig," Tucker observed with a grin as he stepped on the accelerator and let out the clutch. The truck zoomed a short distance over the paved road, then lurched into the bumpy track leading to the hog house. Paul held on to the door handle and braced his feet against the floorboard for support. As the creaking vehicle was bouncing over a series of dry ruts, a brown blur entered Paul's peripheral vision. At the same instant he heard Dundas shout, "Tucker, watch out!"

The blur continued forward, sprang from a mound of rocks, and sailed in front of the truck. Tucker reacted as fast as humanly possible, yet could not hit the brakes or swerve in time to avoid Einstein. There was a loud, crunching *THUMP* as Einstein collided with the radiator grill.

"Oh, Lord," cried Tucker, and Paul's heart sank in his chest. Before he or Tucker could exit the cab, Dundas had jumped from the truck and gone to kneel over the fallen dog.

Paul and Tucker scrambled toward the front of the truck and Dundas said, "He's still breathing. He's alive."

Alive, maybe, but Einstein's front left leg was grossly dislocated at the shoulder and there was blood trickling from his nose. Tucker dropped to his knees and mumbled, "I'm sorry, fellow. I never saw you coming."

"It wasn't your fault," Dundas offered consolingly.

But Tucker, suddenly overwrought with emotion, was not consoled and he snapped, "How could it be my fault? He threw himself in front of the truck."

Paul's heart sank even lower. He hung his head and prayed for a miracle.

"Look," Tucker blurted hopefully. "He opened his eyes."

"Yeah, but . . ." Dundas was choked with agony. "That blood in his nose isn't good. He's ruptured inside."

As if to confirm the fact, Einstein made a gurgling noise in his throat. He then looked at Tucker, Dundas, and Paul. His eyes said he knew he was dying.

Tucker shuddered. "Let's get him in the truck."

"Why?" Dundas asked softly. "He won't make it to the vet."

"No," Tucker replied. "But he loves the truck. That's the best place for him."

"Right," Dundas agreed. "I'll get his head and shoulders, Tucker. You lift his rump. We'll put him up front. Paul, open the door."

Paul did as he was bid and watched through tear-moistened eyes as the men lifted Einstein from the ground and carried him to the truck. Dundas entered the cab backward, lay the dying dog's head gently on the seat and exited through the driver-side door. As he did so, Tucker tenderly placed Einstein's broken leg in its proper position and whispered, "Go easy, boy."

Numb with grief, Dundas, Tucker, and Paul stood silently by the truck avoiding eye contact with one another while waiting for Einstein to die.

But Einstein wasn't ready to die. Not yet. Not before achieving one last desire.

With a final, heroic thrust of energy, Einstein struggled upright in the seat, rested the paw of his good front leg on the dashboard and gazed through the windshield. Although blood dribbled from his nose onto his chest, he stared ahead as any passenger might, apparently admiring the passing world.

"Hennley taught him to ride like that," Tucker said in a cracking voice.

"He loved riding with Hennley," Dundas added grimly.

Then Einstein turned and looked at the three sad humans standing by the truck. He blinked . . . and fell over sideways on the seat. Tucker opened the door and peered into the truck for a long while before saying, "His suffering is over. He's gone to the mystery now."

Dundas groaned as if he'd been punched in the stomach.

Paul bit his bottom lip and wiped tears from each cheek.

For a moment no one moved or spoke; then Tucker reached into the glove compartment and retrieved the vial of antibiotics, which he handed to Dundas. "Here, give Vanessa her medicine. There's a tarp under the seat. Paul and I'll wrap Einstein up and go tell Ellis what happened."

Dundas stepped forward for a last look at the dog, and before turning toward the hog house, told Tucker, "Don't bury him without me."

Tucker and Paul found Ellis in the barnyard, and when Tucker gave him the news, Ellis winced and reached up to cover his heart with his right hand. "Where is he now?"

Tucker gestured toward the rear of the truck.

Ellis stared solemnly at the truck, then shook his head and said, "I better go call Dad. Wait here, will you? We'll figure out where to bury him when I get back."

As Tucker and Paul watched Ellis stride away, Tucker looked at Paul and remarked, "A hell of a last day for you, isn't it?"

"Horrible."

"You have any ideas about burying Einstein?"

Paul was about to shrug and say no when a notion crossed his mind. "Up at the cottage might be good."

Tucker gave Paul an approving look. "Good thinking. Of course, if Ellis agrees, we'll have to get Rebecca's permission. It's her place now, you know."

Paul nodded. He knew.

Tucker crossed his arms and furrowed his brow in thought.

Then Paul — surprising himself more than Tucker — volunteered, "I'll go ask Rebecca if you want. It won't take me ten minutes to run there and back."

Tucker's demeanor did not change. "That'll work. Best to bring her here, though, and I'll ask her. I don't want her feeling we already decided. If her mother gets curious, just say I sent you."

Paul knew he wasn't supposed to address Tucker formally, but he couldn't refrain from doing so before turning and running from the barnyard. "Yes, sir."

"I have no objections, Dad. I think it's wise," Rebecca told her father.

"I didn't think you'd mind," Tucker responded warmly. "Just thought it was right to ask."

"Tucker."

"Yeah, Ellis?"

"How about you drive up to the cottage and pick out a final resting spot? I'll take Rebecca and Paul in my truck and get Dundas."

"Okay."

★ ★ ★ ★ ★

twenty

Rebecca and Paul could hear Dundas talking to Vanessa as they approached the shed in the corner of the compound. "That virus doesn't stand much of a chance now. Not against a strong girl like you," he was saying, then fell silent when he became aware of their presence. He was sitting on a stool, elbows on his knees, chin in his hands, hunched over Vanessa's giant head.

"Hello, Dundas," Rebecca said softly.

Dundas dropped his hands and turned slowly toward Paul and Rebecca. His face was wet with tears and distorted with anguish.

"How is the patient?"

Some of the pain left Dundas's face. He seemed to appreciate the question. "A little better, I think."

"That's wonderful to hear."

Dundas bobbed his head, then drew a deep breath and told Rebecca, "I think when Einstein was missing he figured where to find Hennley . . . and now he's gone there."

"Could be."

The expression on Dundas's face shifted suddenly into a guilty pout and he confessed, "I never saw Hennley's ghost. Hennley never spoke to me either. I just made that up because I missed him so much and no one would ever talk about him."

Paul gave Rebecca a quick look. Her theory about Dundas was proven true.

"We were all sad." Rebecca's voice was full of forgiveness. "I would've talked about him with you, Dundas. We still can someday."

Dundas heaved a gloomy little shrug.

Rebecca lay the fingers of her right hand lightly upon Dundas's shoulder. "We're going to bury Einstein at the cottage. Dad already drove him there. Ellis is waiting outside in his truck."

"You coming, Dundas?" Paul said after the man

showed no sign of responding. "You should be there. It wouldn't be right without you."

"I reckon I should," Dundas said after a pause, and before rising to go with Rebecca and Paul, leaned over to tell Vanessa, "You keep getting better. I'll be back soon."

Rebecca, Ellis, Dundas, and Paul got out of the truck and walked through the swale to where Tucker had parked at the edge of the cottage yard. For an emotionally oppressive moment, everyone hemmed and hawed and looked grimly at the ground. Finally Rebecca asked her father, "Did you find a good spot for Einstein?"

"I did," said Tucker, all eyes following as he gestured toward a lip of land projecting out over the swale. "It's the last place in the yard to get sun every day. He'll rest well there."

As Ellis, Rebecca, and Paul were murmuring their approval, Dundas opened a door in the green truck and reached behind the seat for a shovel. He carried the tool to the chosen ground, outlined a rectangular box and began digging. Everyone gathered around to watch.

Dundas had just finished removing the grassy topsoil from within the marked box when Ellis stepped forward and practically yanked the shovel from his hands. "Here. Let me show you how to dig."

Dundas frowned darkly at Ellis, reluctantly released his grip on the tool, and retreated from the proscribed area.

Then Tucker, after watching Ellis labor for approximately two minutes, stepped forward. "I've seen rain dig holes faster than that. Let me take it from here."

Ellis mumbled a few choice words under his breath before giving up the shovel and going to stand by Dundas.

In the next fifteen minutes the shovel changed hands no less than three more times, and as Paul watched the men pass the implement back and forth, he wondered if he too should vie for the privilege of digging Einstein's grave. He had not known the great dog for as long as the others, but they had been friends. Finally Paul made a move to reach for the shovel, yet just as he did, Dundas brushed past him and assumed the ceremonial tool from Ellis.

Paul saw that Rebecca had withdrawn from the group and gone to sit on the bench. He went over to stand by her and she greeted him with a knowing look. Somehow Paul understood what she was thinking: *By digging the grave, the men are honoring Hennley.*

Then Hargrove's car appeared on the ridge road, drove to the gate, and parked in front of Ellis's truck. The car doors opened and out stepped Granny Furr, Inez Buttons, and Ada and Hargrove Vallenport. Because of Granny's age, Inez's girth, and Hargrove's bum leg, they gathered in a line behind the gate, resigned to witnessing the funeral from afar.

Soon the grave was deemed deep enough and the solemn trio — Tucker, Ellis, and Dundas — trudged to the truck and collected Einstein's wrapped body. They carried the bloodstained bundle to the prepared site and set it gently on the ground by the mound of displaced earth; then Dundas dropped into the hole.

Ellis and Tucker reverently lifted and handed Einstein to Dundas, who lay the dog down to rest forever.

Dundas climbed from the open grave, grabbed the shovel from the mound of earth and, with a show of deference, presented the tool to Tucker.

"Anyone wish to say some final words?"

"Someone should."

"We all should."

"You speak first, Tucker," suggested Ellis. "Then pass the shovel. That way we'll all do him equal service."

At that moment, Rebecca reached out and took

Paul's right hand in hers. He welcomed her touch with a gentle squeeze and clasped her hand.

Tucker took a scoop of dirt from the mound, held it over the open grave and said in a clear, strong voice, "Below us lies the body of Einstein. This farm will never be the same without him. Please, Lord, reserve a soft cloud for our friend to sleep on, and if there are any green pickup trucks in heaven, park one on his cloud."

With a spin of the shovel, Tucker released earth into the grave and handed the tool to Ellis.

Ellis also scooped dirt from the mound and held the shovel over the grave. "The first time I saw Einstein he was small enough to fit in Hennley's hat. Since then, that dog has been closer to my heart than any animal I ever knew. With Einstein goes a part of anyone who ever looked in his eyes and wondered what he was thinking. May he rest in peace forever."

Dundas filled the shovel to full capacity and held it

high over the open grave. He looked skyward, looked at Tucker and at Ellis, then gazed into the burial pit and addressed Einstein's body. "No one ever accused you of being well behaved, but you always thought for yourself and were a credit to your race. You are gone now, but not forgotten."

And at that, Dundas rotated the wooden handle and rained soil down on the much-loved dog.

As Paul stood holding Rebecca's hand, watching the men fill the hole in the world, listening to the muffled sound of falling earth, aware of the mourners at the gate on the far side of the swale, he knew he would remember this day and these people for the rest of his life.

Some understandings are implicit in the experience and cannot be reduced to metaphor. What one learns from the experience becomes personal wisdom, known only to the inner self, and then only in an individually invented vocabulary of codes, symbols, and intuitive connections. Such was Paul Shackleford's understanding of his summer on the Vallenports' farm. The experience meant much to him and he knew what it meant, but he did not try to capture that meaning in words.

Although Paul was glad to see his friends again and, day by day, was increasingly absorbed in the

twenty-one

excitement of a new school year, he spent much of his time musing about Rebecca and Granny and Dundas and the others that remained on the Vallenports' farm. Mostly he mused about Rebecca and the kiss they never shared.

Finally nearly two weeks after leaving the farm, Paul decided to write Rebecca the letter he'd been intending to write since his return home. He was sitting in study hall when he made the decision, but he did not begin the letter there. He wanted to write it on special paper, and to do so, he would first have to stop by the mall on his way home from school and purchase the right stationery.

Rebecca beat Paul to the punch. Her letter was waiting for him when he arrived home from the mall that afternoon.

Although Paul had never before seen anything she had written, the instant he saw his name printed boldly and simply on the envelope, he knew that he was looking at Rebecca Dyson's handi-work.

He sat down at the kitchen table and opened the envelope. The letter was written in purple ink, with just enough feminine flourishes to make it pretty without being distracting.

Dear Paul,

I hope this finds you well. You've probably been too busy with school and all your friends in Richmond to think much of us back here on the farm, but we've thought of you quite often. When Dad heard I planned to write you this letter he asked me to tell you that Inez Buttons has gone on a politeness craze in the kitchen and holds you up as the standard almost every day. He says at the rate Inez is going, they'll be saying yes ma'am to the cows by October.

I have lots of news. First, last Sunday night Dundas walked up to the big house when no one was around, took the keys from the hook in the garage, and drove off in Hennley's old green truck. You probably know the railroad crossing west of the farm. Dundas drove the truck there and parked it on the tracks just before the regular night train came barreling through the gap. Who knows if he stayed to watch what happened, but the train completely destroyed the truck and scattered it in bits and pieces for more than a mile.

Anyway, the funniest thing about the whole story is that Dundas returned the keys to the hook and never told anyone what he'd done. He just went to work the next day and pretended nothing had happened, and no one would have known if Mrs. Vallenport hadn't heard the truck start up and looked out the window in time to see Dundas driving away. It's only a guess, but I think he got tired of the truck reminding him of Hennley and Einstein, and figured out of sight was out of mind.

Now for the big news. Maya and Ellis are engaged to be married next April. Everyone is so happy for them. And by the way, you better start looking for a tuxedo because Maya said they planned to invite you. And speaking of inviting, I visited Granny Furr yesterday and we were talking about this coming Thanksgiving. I don't know if you knew, but everyone always eats in the big house with the Vallenports. Granny said it would only be proper for you to come and stay in your old room. I expect you have plans with your family, but if you don't, you're officially invited here.

It would be good to see you again, Paul. All the boys at my school seem to think hooting and hollering is the best way to impress girls, and I remember that you were always a gentleman when we were together this summer.

Lastly, I remember you saying you had a computer. Well, last week I set up an e-mail address at school. I have access to the computer only on Tuesdays and Thursdays during study hall, but I was thinking it might be a good way for us to stay in touch. If you agree, send me a snail-mail letter with your e-address and I'll send you mine.

Until then, tranquility.

Love,

Rebecca

P.S. I almost forgot. Vanessa made a full recovery the week after you left. Dad saw her the other day and said she has rebounded nicely.

P.P.S. Don't forget to think about Thanksgiving.

Paul reread the letter, then stared at the salutation for a good ten minutes. The word "tranquility" reminded him of Hennley's letter to Rebecca and the advice contained in it, and Paul thought, *The wisdom in my heart says walk to the Vallenports' farm for Thanksgiving if you have to.*

It would not be accurate to say that Paul's eyes filled with tears of happiness, yet they did moisten with joy and were glistening when his father arrived home a little early from work and found him in the kitchen.

"Hello, son. Are you okay?"

"Fine, Dad. Just thinking."

"Oh?"

"Yeah. Remember when you dropped me off at the farm at the beginning of the summer and you told me that saying 'Is the desert to the jungle real?'"

"I do, vaguely. Why?"

"I just figured it out, and the answer is yes. They are different on the surface, but they're real to each other."

Morris hung his jacket on a hook and sat across from Paul. "Care to explain that, son?"

"Naw. Just think about it, Dad. You'll understand."